# Marwan

## The Autobiography
## of a 9/11 Terrorist

Aram Schefrin

authorHOUSE®

*AuthorHouse™*
*1663 Liberty Drive, Suite 200*
*Bloomington, IN 47403*
*www.authorhouse.com*
*Phone: 1-800-839-8640*

*First published by AuthorHouse 11/26/2007*

*ISBN: 978-1-4343-3288-2 (sc)*

*Library of Congress Control Number: 2007906145*

*Printed in the United States of America
Bloomington, Indiana*

*This book is printed on acid-free paper.*

# AUTHOR'S NOTE

This book was written in 2003, and submitted then to a number of publishers in New York. The response it received shocked me – although I probably should not have been shocked.

New York was then caught up in its collective grieving. To write a book about the sacred subject of 9/11 was considered insulting, outrageous and an attempt to profit from misery. Worse than that, the book was written from the terrorists' point of view, presented them as real people and attempted to explain why they had done what they had. There was no room in the minds or hearts of New Yorkers then for anything other than black-and-white condemnations of these men. Those publishers who approached the subject with a bit more sophistication believed that only a Muslim could write a book about what Muslims had done.

Well ... time has passed, and art has begun to deal with 9/11. The information about 9/11 which has come out since 2003 has confirmed that what I wrote was largely correct. So I hope, this time, we're ready to give some serious thought, not just to the victims, but to why 9/11 happened.

We are told that we face a "clash" of civilizations which will color our future for the next hundred years. If this is true – and it may be – it is very important to understand what the other side thinks, and why they think it. We are told the whole thing is a religious matter; that the conflict is therefore inevitable and there's nothing we can do, or ever could have done, to avoid it. That is not true – there is a lot more to it than that.

To defend ourselves against what is considered a deadly opposition, we must understand where it comes from, and where it intends to go. The characters in this book each come with a different perspective; and I believe that I have explored most of the reasons we face what we face. I hope America is now ready to look at the problem seriously. Because if we do not at least try to understand what we face, then if we survive this conflict without paying a great price, it will have been a matter of sheer dumb luck.

To those of you who may be outraged at the cool manner in which these characters plan mass murder, or at the humor I sometimes use, let me say: sociopathic murderers are only a short step away from normal, and may not necessarily be bad dinner company.

This book was extensively researched. I visited all the Florida sites at which the terrorists lived. Much of the detail comes from reports in local Florida newspapers, which used the local angle to probe deeper than the national press. The major events and locations are accurate, though I have used my imagination in describing them, and taken some liberties with the chronology. The supporting players are all fictionalized, although real people did play most of these parts. The behavior and character of each of the hijackers is based on what has been reported about them and their lives, and on (sometimes wide-ranging) inferences I have drawn from that data base.

I know they did the big things that I say they did. The little things are fiction – but I'll bet they are pretty close to the mark.

Aram Schefrin
June, 2007

# 1

**New York City: June, 2000**

*Bi ism 'Allah ar-Rahman ar-Rah'im.*
*In the name of Allah, the Merciful, the Compassionate.*

---

I looked down through a haze of smog from the top of the Empire State. The "greatest city in the world" was an ugly jumble of buildings, for the most part dreary, more like Dickens' London, as I imagined it, than the clean, airy symmetry of the skyline of Dubai. On a rooftop here and there, someone had struggled desperately to create a patch of greenery, to commune with something more pure than the money-worshipping frenzy in the streets down below.

"You see how they build this city? No rules, no plan. Profit is the only thing they think about. So, Marwan – how was your flight?"

The voice was behind me. I turned around. Atta was standing there, with Ziad Jarrah.

1

I had flown in direct from Hamburg; Jarrah had done the same, but on another plane. Atta had taken a bus from Hamburg to Prague, then flown from there to Kennedy. We had agreed beforehand that this was where we would meet. We had already known that al-Shibh had not been able to get a visa. He said he would take care of the problem, though he didn't know what it was. Al-Shibh could wangle anything – so we expected him soon.

Since I had seen them last, Atta and Jarrah had shaved off their beards. Jarrah looked like the typical Western college kid – except a little cleaner, and a lot less loud. His hair was cut close to his head; he might even have razored it. That was the style in America, and Jarrah remembered how to be cool from the days when he had worked at it. Atta said it was all right, because the Prophet had had his head shaved once, and had implored Allah for His mercy on everyone with a shaved head or – like me – with his hair cut short. Atta was wearing a black T-shirt and black Armani jeans. He looked like that guy with the cockatoo in that show "Beretta" that I used to get in Qusaibat on the TV from Dubai.

"The flight was good, cousin. So – here we are."

Atta said: "Do you know why I picked this place to meet?"

"Because you wanted us to see …"

"Everything we hate. Come." We leaned out over the parapet, and Atta showed us where Wall Street was – the fortress of the Yahoodis; the advertising area, where they were always busy making us want what we didn't need; Times Square, home of the Jew press and assorted depravities. He pointed out the bridges that led into the city from the east and the west. "I don't hate those bridges," he said. "George Washington, Throg's Neck. Whitestone. Brooklyn Bridge. They express the nature of God. They are so magnificent, they are almost blasphemous."

And then two tall ugly buildings to the south. Atta hated skyscrapers – people piled on top of each other. "Hideous." He made a face. "Like what goes on inside them. Hey – Marwan. You have to look at them."

But I could not look at them. "It's like seeing your own tombstone. Let's go somewhere else."

Jarrah mugged for the cameras of the fat tourists in jeans and sneakers as we pushed through their sweat stink onto the elevator, holding our breaths until we were disgorged into the street. I had already had enough of New York. No matter where we looked that day, we found filth – not just wrappers and cigarette butts but a coating of grime on everything, which only a flood like Noah's could have cleansed away.

So it was not a high point when Atta led us down some steps into a hole in the sidewalk that smelled like my unwashed laundry did when I let it sit for two weeks. Atta handed me a coin, and I followed him to a turnstile and watched him insert a similar coin into a slot. The turnstile spun as he pushed on

3

it, and let him through. I was about to do the same when three monkeys scrambled down the stairs and leap-frogged over the turnstiles, scattering to the right and left toward places I could not see. This gorilla show so startled me that I dropped my coin – not into the slot but onto the floor, where it rolled on its edge for fifty feet until it stuck in a wad of bubble gum still fresh enough to hold it.

Atta gave me another coin and I forced my way through the turnstile. Suddenly the whole place shook and a train slid into the station. Doors opened and people poured out and slammed me into a pole. Atta yanked me through one of the doors. If he had not, I would not have gone into that car for all the sneakers in China.

I am from desert people. This was not civilized.

Coming up the stairs at the end of the ride, I gasped for air, and then choked on what I had drawn into my lungs. When I finally straightened up, I saw in front of me the bases of two buildings embossed with high narrow arches like a crocheted antimacassar.

"You shit!" I snarled at Atta. "Why did you bring me here?"

"I didn't bring you here," Atta said. "Allah did."

# 2

**Hamburg: November, 1996**

*Bi ism 'Allah ar-Rahman ar-Rah'im*
*Im Namen Allahs, des Gnädigen, des Barmherzigen*

---

The taxiruf driver was Shi'a. From Iran. It took no genius to recognize that. Marwan read his name on the taxi license posted on the back of his seat: Rafsanjani, or something identifiable. There were also calligraphic fragments of Shi'a truth taped all over the dashboard of his Mercedes SUV.

Marwan had told him where he wanted to go. The driver didn't respond. But as they sped away from Hamburg's Hauptbahnhof, where Marwan's train had come in from Bonn, he saw in the rear view mirror that the driver was muttering. And he knew what was going on: the driver was cursing him for a Sunni, as the Shi'a have cursed the Sunni for thirteen hundred years, since the death of the Third Khalifa destroyed the unity of the faith.

5

The imprecations of plagues rolled out of him. They were not original – you might find them on the internet if you searched under "How To Swear in Tehran," or "Farsi Abuse." They were, mostly, disgusting. But Marwan had endured the Shi'a phenomenon often enough that he could take a lot of it before it got his goat.

The light was a glow, like a Rembrandt, and it was bitter cold as they passed down a street of prostitutes. The driver removed his hostile attentions from Marwan and put them onto what they were seeing through the frosted windows: very German *junge nutten*, the boys dressed like Ozzie Osbourne, the girls like Britney Spears, and their mothers – either pimps or whores – like Salvador Dali nightmares of Bardot or Tina Turner. Marwan gave a few of them a lookover – the kids, not the mothers. Not that he would have paid for sex – no, that's not true, he would have. But he was already late. Besides he would be praying soon, if he knew his cousin, and while he had no compunctions about breaking one of Allah's laws, it would be better for all if he did not arrive stinking of woman juice.

They crossed the Elbe in a shivery wind on the B4 heading south, and entered the Harburg suburb on the Grossmoordam. At the address Marwan had given him, the driver slammed on the brakes, throwing Marwan into the seat-dividing glass.

"What kind of way is that to drive?" Marwan howled.

The driver looked out the windshield. "It is the Shi'a way."

"You almost killed me!"

"That was my intention. Apparently it is not yet your time."

Disgusted, Marwan brought his wallet out. "What do I owe you, Shi'a pig?"

"Can you not read the meter, dog?" the driver snarled.

Marwan wanted to hit him, but couldn't, through the glass. "The meter is a liar, like you!"

The driver shrugged. "Pay what you want. I am only sorry you are not dead."

"Open the fucking glass, then, pig."

The driver slid a small partition to the side. Marwan threw bills through it. "Here!"

The driver didn't touch the bills. "I don't want your money."

"No?" Marwan reached through the opening to take the money back.

The driver dropped his hand on the bills, covering them. "If you touch that money, I will put my knife through your hand."

Marwan did not see a knife, but there could have been one. He pulled his hand back through the opening. "Get my suitcase, pig!"

The driver stayed firmly in his seat. "You know where it is. You get it."

Marwan was sick of it. No more arguing. He got out and unloaded his luggage from the boot. As the driver flipped up his meter, and put the pedal to the floor, Marwan heard him pray to Allah that Marwan's head would be cut off and that Marwan would haunt his mother, if Allah let her live, carrying his fucking head in a burlap bag.


Marwan had been in Germany for two years when he had finally convinced himself to make this trip. He was at school miles away, in Bonn, studying *Deutsch*. Well, he was supposed to be. But he never went to class. He already spoke German well, he had learned it on the street. And he had already concluded that he would not need to read in the language. That was a sad decision. But he made it anyway.

The house on the tilting, narrow street was yellowed and falling apart. He hauled his bag up the creaking stairs to the landing outside the flat. When he knocked on the door, Atta tugged it in and stood there with a look that said: "You are here to waste my time."

"You can blame my mother for this," Marwan said.

"Who is your mother?" Atta squinted.

Marwan picked up the suitcase he had set down. "Okay. I was stupid to come."

"Oh. Marwan. No. Come in. I didn't recognize you."

"Why should you? You haven't seen much of me." But Marwan's tone was not pardoning.

He and Atta had not been together for years. Marwan was inches taller now; for the first time, he needed glasses, and his hair had been long when Atta had seen him last – he had cut it short in Bonn. So he was not surprised that Atta didn't know him by sight. Still, he had called to say he was coming. He wasn't just dropping in.

In his youth, you could have described Atta – if you subscribed to the modern view – as attractive, or presentable, in a lantern-jawed sort of way. Now he was as thin as a rail and his beard was down to his chest, having grown as Allah intended it to. He was dressed in the jalbab and the turban, which one did not see much in the West. That day he was haggard and shabby, since he hadn't slept. And his eyes – which had always been fervent – were blacker and deeper set, and threw off a dark light Marwan had never seen before.

The salon, or what you might call it, was bare of decoration. Only a round table surrounded by seven chairs took up any of the space between the little efficiency kitchen and the other three walls of the flat. Oh, and there was a TV too, and a VCR, but Marwan didn't notice them then, since they were off.

"That's a pretty big suitcase," Atta said. What he meant by that was: How long do you plan to stay?

The apartment was not tidy, and that was not like Atta; he had always been neat, Marwan's mother had said, to the point, may be, of obsession. His laptop was on the table, hot from overuse, amidst raggedy piles of Post-It notes in his crabbed German hand and plates of gnawed-upon Sacher tortes and a kind of jelly donut Germans call a Berliner. Atta was walking toward the table. Marwan was following him.

"I have to finish my thesis," Atta said. "It isn't a good time ..."

Atta had worked hard at school since he had been a child. He had had very few friends, and no relations with girls. After class, he would come home quickly and study into the night. It was said that his father had timed the walk home, to keep him from dawdling.

"If this isn't a good time," Marwan said, "why did you say I could come?"

*"'See ye not that I pay out full measure, and provide the best hospitality?'"*

Marwan was more than skeptical. "You call this hospitality?"

"You want a Sacher torte?"

Marwan scanned the debris on the table. "Do you have a Sacher torte that you haven't eaten half of?"

"Maybe. Look in the minifridge." Marwan did look in the minifridge. There were no fresh tortes. He sat at the table across from Atta with a bad case of pastry-envy.

"Tell me what is going on with you," Atta said. But then he lifted the screen of his laptop and gazed into it.

Well, cousin, Marwan thought; here's what's going on. I am walking up the streets of rich neighborhoods in Bonn, or down the leafy *strasses* of the bourgeoisie, trying to understand how these people, who have everything, had instinctively comprehended the secret of how to get it. So far I have not caught on. In the end, on these winter nights, I find a girl in a discotheque who knows even less than I do and won't cost me anything – not even a bratwurst or a bottle of slivovitz. She asks me to take her to my flat. It's not that she tells me why – but I know she wants to catch a glimpse of how Muslims live, and get a taste of the Muslim method of making love. She will learn that it's no different from what she already knows – there used to be artless fumbling, but not any more. If she likes me, she will do it again. If not, she'll say goodbye.

No, Marwan didn't tell this to Atta. He couldn't have.

The little he knew of Atta he did not like. But his mother had insisted he visit to pay his "respects." The al-Haniyyahs (Marwan's family) were poor relations for whom the Attas had never had time. Marwan had not taken it personally, since the Attas had seemed to have little time for anyone but themselves.

The al-Haniyyahs lived in Qusaibat, in the emirate of Ras al Khaimah, a pimple on the hide of Saudi Arabia. The Attas lived in Cairo, in Abdin, a once elegant district which, over the past twenty years, had slipped into disrepair. They never came to visit the al-Haniyyahs. The al-Haniyyahs had only gone to visit them when Marwan's mother went crazed with resentment – which happened once a year – over the loss of the citified freedom and the comfort she had surrendered when she left her home in Egypt to marry Marwan's father, whose only claim to attention from anyone in the world was his post as part-time muezzin at the mosque next door to their house.

11

She hated Ras al Khaimah. But Marwan's life had been comfortable, when he was a boy. He couldn't say he had lacked for anything. His father had had no business sense and never earned enough, and Qusaibat was not a place to brag about; but the oil money trickled down onto everyone in the Emirates, even the Bedu in their tents on the edge of the Empty Quarter. Mostly, it was a tranquil life; you did what was expected – did your schoolwork, did your chores, enjoyed the sand and the sea. You prayed five times a day: at dawn, at noon, at mid-afternoon, at the sunset and after twilight. You fasted at Ramadan. You made a living in some kind of trade; you would do well if you were a talker. You did nothing out of the ordinary unless the preacher said you might. Down the road, if you were obedient, you would likely expect a tranquil death and an eternity in Paradise at Allah's feet.

But, if you studied hard and had earned your parents' trust, there was a secret life for a daring boy at night in Ras al Khaimah. There were girls who would meet you secretly, without a chaperone. All you had to do was get out of your house, and that was not so difficult, because your parents lived a hard life and went to bed at an early hour. These girls would wait for you under a bush at the edge of town. They would let you touch them, although they would not touch you. You had no fear in Ras al Khaimah, like the Saudis had, that a vice patrol Jeep would catch you and lay the whip on you; so you could remove her blouse and bra and lay them aside, and gaze

12

at her little brown nipples and puzzle out what to do with them from the subtle hints you had picked up from *Dallas* and *Dynasty*. She would let you lie on top of her and grind yourself into her. She would laugh at you when your pants got wet, until you got so mad that you would pull her skirt out from under her and pull her panties down and touch her until she stopped laughing and sighed words of love. But that was always the end of it – as far as the game would go. No one would know, to look at her, what she had let you do … but go further and you would ruin her; if her father didn't kill her, she would suffer for the rest of her life. So you would help her pull her panties up and put on her bra and her blouse; then you would sit three feet away from her and she and you would look up at the sky, waiting for Allah's lightning to burn you to a crisp.

Leaving aside the secret nights, Marwan was still a serious boy. He wanted to do something meaningful with his life. But he could not find anything meaningful in the Emirates. They created nothing significant; they had no hefty thoughts. He had gone to a secular school, not a madrassa; he knew English and mathematics – he could do calculus. He had all the necessary tools – but he had nowhere to use them. There were no possibilities – only the things that had always been – for a smart boy in Ras al Khaimah whose father was nobody.

On TV he had seen the Western world full of ingenuity. Every day there was something new which promised to change the future of the whole human race. He thought he might go into medicine, which was bringing us closer and closer to immortality; or something to do with the internet, which could someday become the means by which anything anyone knew or thought could be known to everyone. He had heard that German universities were offering scholarships to smart boys in the Emirates; apparently they had concluded that Arabs might be good for something besides sweeping their streets. He studied hard, he read everything, and after a year of effort he won a scholarship for himself.

When he came to Germany, he was eighteen years old. It was not what he had expected. It broke his heart. This is what he told Atta, even though he didn't like him. He had had no one he could talk to since he had left the Emirates; and for Arabs, that's what cousins are for – and they are required to listen, even if they don't care.

It had not taken Marwan long to understand that the masters of technology in the West were less interested in improving the human lot than in the money they were piling up in staggering, obscene quantities. And once they had the money, what did they do with it? Ostentations, perversions, useless *accoutrements*, mindless diversions, one-up-manship.

Atta nodded distractedly, his eyes on the laptop screen: *"'The unbelievers spend their wealth to hinder man from the path of Allah ....'"*

What they did was for their own glory, Marwan said, not to help the world. They had ideas, but no humanity. "I can't be part of that. I can't work for them. I don't care about money – really, I don't! But now, I mean, I don't know what to do … Okay, I know, you're laughing. It's ridiculous."

But that was when Atta first looked up from the laptop screen. *"'So when thou art empty, labor, and let thy Lord be thy Quest,'"* he said.

"Well," said Marwan, squirming under Atta's now-watchful eye. "I'm boring anyway. What about you?"

Atta tossed an arm toward the table. "You see my life. But you should have come to see me sooner."

"How could I? You were not here."

"Well, that is true."

Atta had disappeared from Hamburg a year and half before. It was only a month since he had returned and moved into this flat. "Where did you go?" Marwan asked him. His mother had said no one knew.

Marwan saw Atta thinking about whether he ought to answer. Then, with a quick shake of his head, he said: "I went to Afghanistan."

"The happy land of the Taliban? They could use an architect."

"It was not for that kind of business …."

"Then why did you go?"

The dark light was rising in Atta's eyes. "Do you really want to know?"

"If I don't want to know something, usually I don't ask."

15

"I went to Sheikh Usama. To make jihad."

"You?" Marwan grinned. That was not what he would have expected. Atta was religious, yes; he had been holy, Marwan's mother had said, since he was thirteen. But he had been a shy and sensitive boy. Seraphic, virginal, delicate. His father had called him "Bulbul," "nightingale." Told Atta's doting mom that the child had better toughen up if he were to face the world.

"What do *you* know?" Atta spluttered.

Marwan conciliated. "But I want to know." And, strangely, Marwan realized that that was true.

Atta grimaced. He didn't say anything. Marwan thought he wasn't able to explain himself. But then, in a trickle at first, he began to get it out.

"I went back to Cairo, three years ago, for an urban planning project ... I study urban planning ..."

"Yes." Marwan nodded. "My mother told me that."

"Really? Your mother talks about me?" Atta was startled; seemed actually pleased.

"You are the shining example I am supposed to measure up to."

"Hmm," Atta mused. "That's very nice. Are you measuring up?"

"If I were, she wouldn't talk about you. She would talk about me."

"Keep working at it," Atta grinned. "It's not unattainable."

"The urban planning project ...." Marwan restarted him.

"I was researching a paper on the renovation of the old city gates. I saw what they were doing. It was not renovation. Mubarak – *ibn haram!* - he was tearing down houses and factories to make a tourist attraction. And where were the people who lived there and worked there supposed to go? He had actors wearing painted rags to play the part of the peddlers he had driven out of there! I could have killed Mubarak for that. I wanted to take a gun …" He slipped into silence again.

"But you didn't, obviously."

"No, I didn't do anything. Not then … I went to Aleppo, in Syria. That's what my thesis is about, a place called Khareg Bab-en-Nasr – it's an ancient part of Aleppo they are overdeveloping now. These planners, they don't understand. They only think about concrete. They don't think about the soul. The outer and the inner world must be harmonized in the city, so the city helps the people to live in unity with Allah … You don't know what I'm talking about."

"I think I do," Marwan offered.

"But you don't. Anyway – the Muslim Brotherhood is very strong in Aleppo. I met a man there, they call him Abu Ilyas. He is an export-import trader there, and here in Hamburg, too. I said I had finally seen enough. I was ready to do something."

"What do you mean, 'something'?"

"That's what he asked me. I said I would do *anything*."

"What do you mean, 'anything'?"

17

"Any thing."

"Because of what you saw at the Cairo city gates?"

Atta snapped impatiently: "Do you think that is who I am? That I want to go to make jihad because of one barbarity? I have seen a million barbarities! This was just the thing that smashed the camel's back. No – I was always meant to do it. I just didn't know."

He leaned forward and stared at Marwan with his razor eyes. "When I flew back to Cairo, The Doctor's car picked me up and brought me over to see him."

Marwan asked: "Who is The Doctor?"

Atta smiled and shook his head. "I won't say his name. He was in charge of Islamic Jihad in Egypt at that time."

"Why do they call him The Doctor?"

"Because he *was* a doctor, until he gave up his practice to make jihad. Anyway, he knew who I was – I mean, he had heard of me. He wanted to know about my faith. He asked a lot of questions. Then he said he would call me if there were something I could do. I was thinking of something in Egypt. Something against Mubarak. I knew nothing of Sheikh Usama then. He was in the Sudan.

"I came back to Hamburg. I was taking classes. Two years later, The Doctor called, and I went to Cairo again. I will not tell you what I did there. But I proved myself."

"Wasn't that when the tourists were killed ….?"

Atta grinned. "No guessing! I hid in Cairo a few months;

then The Doctor sent me a plane ticket, Cairo to Karachi. From Karachi I was smuggled into Afghanistan. The Taliban were in control by then. They had given Sheikh Usama a home after the Americans made the Sudanese kick him out. And, when I got there, The Doctor was there, too. The Egyptians had joined with the Sheikh to make jihad, not just in Egypt, but in every Muslim state. That was good for Islam, because the Sheikh is a sweet man, like a Buddhist monk. He is in the world and yet not. You never know what to make of him. He never looks you in the eye. But The Doctor is made of steel.

"I was with him and Sheikh Usama when they made the fatwa against the Americans, and when they bombed the American embassies in Africa. I was still there when Clinton fired missiles at the Sheikh's training camps – but I wasn't where he put them, and neither was Sheikh Usama."

Then, with those piercing eyes, Atta dissected Marwan. The feeling Marwan had was unnerving, like a hot hand twisting his gut. Then Atta dropped his eyes and looked at his watch, and Marwan felt released.

"No more stories," Atta said. "It's time for salat-ul-Maghrib."

The door to the flat crashed open, and a man, dressed entirely in black, whose face was blank except for the cobra-like attitude his drooping eyelids gave him, stalked across the apartment without acknowledging Marwan. He disappeared into a bedroom, returned a moment later with a prayer rug

– not a cheap Belgian janamaz but an old red Afghani baluch, which he laid on the floor and smoothed out with reverent sweeps of his palm. He stood and closed the window blinds; then he slipped through another door, after Marwan heard splashing water, and knew he was preparing himself with the ritual ablution.

When he came back out, he turned to Atta, pointed to Marwan and said: "Who?"

"My cousin, Marwan," Atta said.

"Let him prepare himself."

Marwan didn't know his name yet, but it was Ramzi al-Shibh.

Marwan went into the little bathroom, in which he found nothing personal. He looked his clothes over carefully to make certain they were clean. He said Bismillah, which one says at the beginning of anything, and which means that one does what one does in Allah's name. Then he washed his hands to the wrists three times, rinsed out his mouth three times (his toothbrush was packed in his bag). He three times sniffed water into his nose out of the palm of his hand, then washed his whole face three times, then each arm three times to the far end of the elbow, beginning with the right. He wiped his head with a wet hand, wiped his ears in the manner commanded, washed his feet three times up to the top of the ankles. When he came out, a third man was there, out of breath.

"Sorry I'm late! Shit!" he said. "Class went overtime." The

man was also dressed in black – a jalbab and Calvin Klein jeans. He grinned at Marwan. "I'm Bahaji. You are Atta's cousin, yes?"

Atta said to Marwan: "He lives here, too."

There was a twinkle in Bahaji's eye as he vanished into the washroom. Marwan heard the faucet splash; and then Bahaji came out.

Al-Shibh looked disgusted. He snapped at Bahaji: "You could not have done it properly in that amount of time."

"I did," Bahaji said, irate. "Come on, the sun is going down!" He took a stance on the prayer rug and looked expectantly at the others.

"We have not washed ourselves yet," said Atta, shaking his head.

"Okay, okay!" Bahaji shrugged. "How was I supposed to know?"

Al-Shibh tapped his temple. "Inti mafish mukh. Nothing in his head." He walked into the bathroom and closed the door behind him.

Bahaji went ballistic, though he did not move. "Kuss umak akho sharmuta! Some day I am going to kick his ass!"

"I don't think so," Atta said. "He'll kill you first."

Bahaji waved the warning off. "Aaa. That one is crazy."

"Perhaps," Atta nodded, "but he is entitled to respect."

Al-Shibh came out of the bathroom; Atta went in. Al-Shibh lined himself up with Bahaji on the prayer rug. He stared at Bahaji. Bahaji at first stared back, but could not match al-Shibh's potency, and dropped his eyes. Al-Shibh waved at Marwan impatiently. Marwan walked briskly to the prayer rug and took the place next to him. When Atta came out of the bathroom, al-Shibh called the iqama: "Allah-hu akhbar! Allah-hu akhbar. Ash-hadu anlah il Laha il Allah …" and they said the prayer that had to be said before the sun had set.

# 3

---

We stayed in a small hotel near the 59th Street Bridge. Atta had meetings to go to. Jarrah went out with him – not to the meetings, as far as I knew, but to walk the streets of Manhattan ogling pretty girls. I stayed in the hotel room, except to accomplish the one mission Atta had given me: to go to the public library, get on the internet and find out the hours for prayer in the eastern American time zone.

I adored Jarrah. He was an easy, smiling boy, always full of fun. He had come to Germany at the same time as I had, from al-Marj in the Lebanon, where his family lived – rather well, from what Jarrah had told me. His father was a bureaucrat, and his mother taught. They made – or had – enough money to send him to private school; they were Christian schools, in fact, the best in Lebanon. He had seen much more of Western life than all the rest of us. He had a Turkish girlfriend who lived in Bochum, on the Ruhr River, near Essen, and was learning to be a doctor at the university there. While he had been in Germany, he had spent every weekend with her. He loved her a lot, he said.

He had learned German in Griefswald; then, in 1998, he had moved to Hamburg to study *flugzugbau* – aircraft design – at the University of Applied Science, the *Fachhochschule*. I think he would have built planes if he had not met al-Shibh and Atta. After he met them, that was the end of that. He gave up studying *flugzugbau*; he spent his days at Atta's flat, reading the Qur'an, though he slept in his own rented room in the house of a German widow. Why had he let them change him? He didn't really know – but he was sure that at the end he would find that he had gone the right way.

We rented a car, a blue Ford Taurus, drove cautiously to Newark – the traffic gave me a headache – and put Jarrah on a plane to Sarasota, Florida with a suitcase full of polo shirts and khaki pants. In Sarasota, Jarrah would hire a car and drive down the state's west coast some twenty miles or so to Venice, the home of the flight school he had been registered for. Though Atta and I had been allowed to stay together, it was forbidden to the three of us to train in the same location. Atta and I were going to Norman, Oklahoma. We did not expect to see Jarrah for at least six months.

A few days after Jarrah left, Atta and I hit the road. Oklahoma was thirteen hundred-odd miles away. Atta planned to drive straight through.

Pennsylvania. Ohio. Indiana. Illinois. Missouri – I mean, how many trees can you look at? How many red barns and white farmhouses? How many this, how many that, all the same same same? I had never before been in a place where nothing was interesting.

Atta kept playing CD's he had burned off the internet – suras from the Qur'an, hadiths he was keen on, sermons of Sheikh al-Hawali, and Sheikh Usama's fatwas of two years before: "Praise be to Allah, who says in His Book: '… *then fight and slay the pagans wherever ye find them, seize them, beleaguer them, and lie in wait for them …*'; and peace be upon our Prophet, Mohammed bin-'Abdullah, who said: '*I have been sent with the sword between my hands to ensure that no one but Allah is worshipped …*'"

Outside of Indianapolis, Atta was falling asleep behind the wheel. I slipped Sheikh Usama's CD out and pushed in Rachid Taha. The hard rock Algerian chaabi blasted out of the speakers. Atta stiffened an index finger and jabbed at the "Eject" button. "We do not play music!"

"They told us to play music …"

"That is for when infidels are around. Not for riding in cars."

But, I thought, it woke you up, and if you like, you could dance to it.

We pulled off the road as the dawn came up, and prayed in the breakdown lane. When we were done, I took the wheel.

A few hours later we crossed the Oklahoma border. I had read that the Yankees had stolen this land from the Native American Indians. Beyond the bug-smeared windshield, it had a look I liked.

But Norman was such a *little* town. There was nothing there but the campus of the University of Oklahoma, and students I saw on the streets looked asleep – like there was nothing on their minds. I knew I would come to hate the place, and I would have to be here six long months while we learned to fly.

We took a room at the Travelodge; the flight school had recommended it. The front of the motel was shaped like an Alpine chalet, but the back of the building swelled out like the tiz of an overweight woman. There was a Wal-Mart Super Center nearby, and we wandered through it; but it was everything wrong with America – piles of things no one needed, until convinced otherwise. We ate at a place called The Waffle House, where potatoes swam in thick grease until they gave up and drowned; then we staggered back to the motel room where we said the last salat of the day, I took off my pants and shoes and fell asleep with the lights bright, while Atta made coded cell phone calls and the TV played *Ally McBeal*.

# 4

**Hamburg: November, 1998**

---

As soon as the salat was done, Bahaji regained his humor. "We should leave the prayer rug down for Marwan to sleep on tonight."

Atta snapped: "Are you crazy?"

"It's a joke," Bahaji sighed. "Don't you remember those?"

Marwan could have informed Bahaji that Atta had never told jokes.

The joke was not that Marwan would sleep on the floor, because he had expected to. The bedrooms were occupied by Atta, al-Shibh and Bahaji, and everyone else who came to the flat was required to bunk on the floor. The joke was that they would allow him to sleep on the prayer rug. He would not have done it. He didn't need it anyway. There was a thick gray wall-to-wall carpet which, he could tell from its varying shades, they tried very hard to keep clean. That was impossible. It was much too old.

Al-Shibh and Bahaji went into their own rooms. Atta slapped the TV on, and then the VCR. It cut into the midst of a sermon by an imam in a white robe. His finger stabbed at the camera. "Jews should have their throats cut! They are filthy apes!"

"Have you called your mother lately?" Atta was searching for supper among the relics of Sacher tortes. Holy he may have always been, but he had a taste for sweets.

"I went to see her," said Marwan.

"In Qusaibat?"

"In Egypt."

"I thought you lived in the Emirates … "

"She moved from Ras al Khaimah. After my father died. She says she feels more at home now in the country where she was born."

"Oh, yes, I forgot about that. I loved your father."

"Did you." Well, he may have thought he did, but Marwan doubted it. "She tried to stop me from coming back to Germany. She said she would get a bank loan to support me while I looked for a job. I said I could look until the Last Day, there wouldn't be any good jobs in Egypt."

"Until they shoot Mubarak," Atta spat.

"I went to see your father too." Who still lived in the apartment where Atta had grown up, though these days the place had gone to seed – much like Atta's father – and the windows looked out on tumbledown poverty.

Atta looked startled. "I spoke to him. He never said he saw you."

"I don't think my visit made his day. He probably forgot."

Atta shook his head ruefully. "It's not that he forgets – it's that he doesn't understand. He believes in Mubarak. He believed in Sadat. He believed in the peace with the Jews. I still love him, but he's a pathetic old man."

Then Bahaji burst out of his bedroom. "Let's go to Sharky's," he called.

Atta wouldn't hear of it. "I don't go there anymore."

Al-Shibh threw open the door to his room. "And neither should you, Bahaji. It's haram." Forbidden.

Bahaji's eyes flashed, and his face turned red. "The Prophet said – blessed be he – *'I do not find anything forbidden to eat, if one wants to eat thereof, unless it be carrion, or blood poured forth, or the flesh of swine …'*"

"It's not just the food, Bahaji. It is forbidden because it's American …"

"Eyreh be afas seder umak!" Bahaji retorted sharply.

Marwan meandered close to Bahaji, whom he knew right away he would like. Bahaji's anger was as exuberant as his playfulness had been.

Marwan asked him: "What is this Sharky's?"

"It's a billiard parlor," Bahaji whispered. "An American chain. It's in a Muslim neighborhood. We don't play billiards.

We just like the food. We used to go there all the time, Atta and me. But Atta has not set foot in it since he came back to Hamburg."

"Well, that doesn't surprise me," Marwan was surprised to hear himself say. Because although Atta was not the young man Marwan had known him to be, Marwan did not understand, yet, what he had become.

"Atta's different, isn't he. More like al-Shibh every day. He's ... I can't describe it ... he's so ... like ... *intense!* I mean, al-Shibh is from the Hadhramaut, like Sheikh Usama's father. But Atta is from Egypt, and even the Brothers allow themselves an earthly pleasure there."

Now Marwan had some inkling of what al-Shibh was about. The Hadhramaut was not all that far from Ras al Khaimah. It's a barren land in south Yemen, between the Indian Ocean and the Rub al Khali desert. In the time before Islam, the pagans had called it "The Holy Land." Some of the men who had grown up there had been completely possessed by God. Or by gods, in the old days. Now by Allah.

Bahaji escaped to his bedroom. "Leave it up to Atta," he grumped, "and you won't eat tonight." And he was right. Marwan didn't.


Two o'clock in the morning. A hand was shaking him. Al-Shibh was squatting over him, with explosive eyes.

"I saw how you prayed, fajir," he hissed. "You are out of

the habit. What is the matter with you? You don't believe in Islam, jahili?" Unbeliever. "You don't believe in Allah? Bah!" He threw out a scornful hand. " *'Surely man waxes insolent, for he thinks himself self-sufficient.'* Do you know what the Qur'an promises to Muslims who slip?"

From that angle, al-Shibh was terrifying – well, from any angle, he was a frightening man – and Marwan knew it would not be safe to confirm him in what he had said. Al-Shibh was not completely correct, but his highly-tuned Islamic nose had smelt out something suspicious.

Marwan had begun to pray, as the hadith requires, at the age of seven. By the time he was ten, Marwan often took his father's place in the next-door minaret when papa was ill or off on some of his insignificant business. Marwan chanted the prayers beautifully; he knew them all by heart. Sung, the poetry of the Qur'an is so gorgeous you want to cry. It makes you believe in Allah, because only Allah could have uttered words that have so much magic in them.

Marwan had been a believer; but he wasn't any more. The magic had no effect on him now. He had had enough of it. That's what al-Shibh had realized, watching Marwan pray.

Al-Shibh had a book in his hand. He was going to throw it at Marwan, but caught himself, kissed it and laid it on Marwan's chest. "You had better read this Qur'an! You little scum!"

At that, he rose and faded into the night's indiscriminate

shade. Marwan was back to sleep in five seconds, giving al-Shibh not a moment's thought.

But when he opened his eyes at the first ray of light, al-Shibh was standing over him. He certainly had al-Shibh's attention. He had no idea why.

"Well? Did you read it?" al-Shibh glared.

Marwan got up, said "Good morning," and stumbled away from him.

Al-Shibh picked the book up from the floor. "I asked you a question. Did you open this Qur'an? Don't lie. I was watching you."

As was the habit of many Yemeni, al-Shibh was chewing the leaves of a shrub called *qat* which – Marwan knew since he had tried it – worked on you like cocaine.

"Isn't it time for prayers?" Marwan said.

"You are filthy. Go get clean."

After the others had appeared – Bahaji full of energy, Atta dragging himself – and after the prayers were said at dawn, al-Shibh cornered Marwan. While the others went about their business, he pinned Marwan to a wall.

"What do you think of America?"

"Well …" Marwan gathered a thought or two. "I think I envy them."

"Yes? And why is that?"

"Because Americans can do whatever they want."

"And what if what they want to do is very bad for you?"

"I don't know what you're talking about."

"America has soldiers in the holiest lands of Islam. In Mecca and Medina. That doesn't bother you?"

It didn't bother Marwan, because it wasn't true. "They are not in Mecca and Medina, I don't think. They are out in the desert." He saw a fury cross al-Shibh's face which was quickly repressed.

"They are in Arabia. They are close enough. But I see you are not concerned about that."

"The Saudis invited them …"

"The Saudis? Not the Saudis! The House of Saud!" The fury was inching back up in al-Shibh, but now it was not aimed at Marwan.

"Because Saddam Hussein invaded Kuwait …"

"Yes – as if that matters! When the corrupt attack the corrupt, it is Allah who wins. If the Saudis needed help, they could have called on the Afghani mujahidin. We destroyed the Soviets, we could have massacred Saddam. But the royal family panicked and brought in the Americans. Then they boasted of the weapons they had bought – spy planes, and fighter jets. And yet they could not defend themselves, and I will tell you why – because the money to buy those weapons wound up in the pockets of the House of Saud!"

Al-Shibh's face was purple. He was going apoplectic. "They left all the decisions to the Americans. They would have run away, if the worst came to the worst. The Americans came, and they don't leave. So who are the real kings of Arabia? Kuf'rs – infidels! But what do you care about that?!"

"The Americans came to protect Kuwait …"

"The Americans came to hold their hands on the oil! What do they care for Kuwaitis? My God, I have to calm myself! But you drive me to distraction!" He bent his head down and his chest sank in. In a while, he straightened up. "I am sorry you do not understand that it is the greatest offense to Islam that kuf'rs are allowed into the lands of the Prophet, peace be upon him. Since the Prophet – blessed be he – chased out the Jews and the Christians, no kuf'r set foot in Arabia until Saud invited the British in to help him drive out the Hashemites. And then, when oil was discovered, he brought everybody in! Why did the Arabs not learn to find the oil themselves? And to bring it up, and build pipelines and refineries, and carry it to the rest of the world and sell it in Arab gas stations?"

Marwan was not – yet – taking this seriously; but that was a very good question, as it seemed to him.

Al-Shibh said: "I will tell you why not. For a thousand years Islam ruled the world. We were the center of power, of science, of art, of philosophy, when America was unheard of and Europe was a piddling puddle of shit. And then something happened. We lost our faith. Allah had abandoned us, because we had abandoned Him. The Devil allied with the West; the West, with his help, grew, and we did not. We did not know how to find the oil because we did not know how to know.

"And, of course, the West defeated us. They walked in and took what they wanted. We were colonized, stolen from, raped. And we admired them for it! We thought if we imitated them, we could make ourselves strong again. And what did that foolishness bring us? Nothing but misery – corrupt regimes like Mubarak's, like Saddam's; military disasters; the worst kind of poverty; dependency on infidels; the destruction of the old ways that served us so well for so long, of our relationship with Allah and life in God's True Path. And despite our adopting Western ways, still we are held in contempt!

"And so now it is the Americans who occupy us; they plunder our riches, they rule our rulers. They terrorize us; they murder us – they killed a million in Iraq! Half of them were children! And in Bosnia …"

"They *helped* us in Bosnia …" Marwan pointed out.

"In Chechnya …"

"That was the Russians …"

"In Palestine …"

"The Israelis …"

"What are you, an idiot?" al-Shibh roared. "Who arms the Israelis? Who says everything they do is just fine? Don't you know that the Jews own America? The newspapers, the colleges, the movies, the TV? You cannot be that stupid that you don't know! America is the mother of Israel!"

Al-Shibh was silent a moment, and then he smiled. He was so unused to smiling that his face found it difficult. "A moment ago you used a word …"

"A word?" Marwan said.

"The word 'us.' 'They helped *us* in Bosnia,' you said. That is interesting." He paused for so long that Marwan thought al-Shibh was through with him. But then he leaned toward Marwan. "What we used to be, and what we are now … does *that* bother you? That we were a great people, and now are contemptible shit …?"

Suddenly he reached out and grabbed Marwan's shoulders, hard. "We are not meant to be contemptible! What does Allah say? '*You are the best nation ever brought forth to men, bidding to honor, and forbidding dishonor, and believing in God.*' Do you understand, Marwan? The law is prescribed by God, not by man. These Christians, they are not governed by God, as much as they speak of Him. But, for us, Allah is everything! And that is why we are the ones who must rule the world! This is not only logical; it is Allah's command. And there is no way around it. We must do what He wants us to do!"

Al-Shibh had exhausted himself. He let Marwan go. Marwan didn't get to respond to him. But if al-Shibh had stopped to listen, Marwan would have said that he didn't want to rule the world. He just wanted a place in it.

# 5

**Norman, Oklahoma; Sarasota, Florida;
Venice, Florida: June, 2000**

---

The office of the flight school, at the Westheimer Airport in Norman, was in a box of a building I have to describe as nondescript. A fat blonde girl with a hard face sat at a metal desk surrounded on every wall by hundreds of photographs, each of them in the same black frame, of people who must have been students, standing next to planes. Some day my photo might go up there. I wondered what they would do with it after they heard the news. They could put it up on eBay, make a couple of bucks – if they had not been imprisoned for educating me.

"Hey!" I said to the blonde girl. "Me and my friend, we want to learn to fly the big jets."

"Yeah?" She blinked. "Do you know how to fly the little ones?"

I said: Nope. We didn't. Not yet.

She stood up, snapped her gum and disappeared out the back. A moment later a big man with bright white hair and a belly that smothered his belt buckle burst in from wherever she had gone to and thrust out a beefy hand. "How y'all?" he said loudly. "What kin I do fer ya?"

Atta disdained the hand. "We want …" he began.

"Yeah, we get lots of Saudis. Wanna fly for Saudia Airlines. I assume, if you're like the rest of 'em, you don't know nothin' yet."

I nodded. "A fair assumption."

"Well, gotta start at the beginning, and this is the place to do it. We fly Cessnas and Pipers, IFR equipped, but the good thing about Norman is we get over three hundred days of VFR weather here. The course fee's twenty-two thousand – each – and we guarantee you'll leave here with all the skills you're gonna need, and all the paperwork, and we won't charge ya a dollar more no matter how long it takes ya."

"Can we see the airplanes?" Atta asked.

"Ya sure can, but if you don't know nothin' about 'em, I don't see the point."

Atta's eyes flashed. Somehow, since he had removed his beard, they had become more threatening. "The point is that we don't want to die flying some piece of garbage."

"Y'know," the big man drawled back, "I think this ain't gonna work out."

"Okay. We'll go to Florida," Atta muttered to me.

That was more like it – Florida: familiar palms everywhere; the turquoise Gulf of Mexico, so like our own; Sarasota, so Arabian, a clean pastel city on a bright white beach.

When Atta had called for instructions after things fell apart in Norman, he had been given the name of a flying school at the Sarasota airport. As soon as we hit Sarasota, we made for the school. We walked out on the tarmac, broiling the soles of our feet.

The instructor was young and slim, with slicked black hair and eyes hidden behind a pair of Raybans. He leaned against what he told us was a Cessna C-152. It was a flimsy-looking thing. It scared me half to death.

"This plane here is easy to fly; it's what we'll teach you on. It's a hundred and ninety hours from git to go, thirty-five first on the private pilot course, which is twenty dual, fifteen solo, five on the ground – with the Jeppesen kit, med exam and flight test that's just about three grand. Then there's eighty-five solo in the 152, that's forty one hundred bucks …"

"What are you giving me prices for?" Atta snarled. "What do you think, I can't pay because I'm a foreigner? You think I sneaked into your country over the Mexican border?"

The instructor took his sunglasses off. His eyes were narrowed down. "Oh, hell, no, that ain't what I think. You Ay-rabs got all the fucking money in the world, ain't I right about that?"

Atta cooled off, and nodded. "Okay. We will do it, whatever it costs."

The instructor slid the glasses up the bridge of his nose. "Let's take a plane ride, buddy, see how your instincts are. My name's Keith, by the way. You?"

"You can call me Mr. Atta."

We climbed into another plane, a C-172, because the 152 was a two-seater and I could not have come along. Atta climbed into the left-hand front seat, Keith took the right. I had two seats to myself in the back.

Keith ran through his checklist, then started the engine up. He moved the plane onto the taxiway, then onto runway 22. I thought he would call the tower – but there wasn't one. Keith pushed up the throttle, and we gained speed; when he pulled back the yoke, the plane lifted off and climbed into clear blue sky.

We banked out and over the gulf, then flew toward the south just to the seaward side of the beach. I had never been in a small plane before. Looking out the front of the plane disconcerted me. There was nothing out the window but a few puffy clouds. I felt as if I were in a taxicab that had taken leave of its senses.

When he leveled off at his altitude, Keith pointed at Atta and took his hands off the stick. For a while, Atta was frozen, so he did nothing at all. But when the plane dropped into a pocket, Atta grabbed the yoke and began to twist it side to side, like people I have seen driving cars in very old movies. The plane began to yaw a bit, and Keith dropped a hand on

Atta's arm as a cautionary signal. Atta smacked the hand away. "Don't ever touch me!"

Keith turned red, and his cheeks bulged. "I don't like you either, bud. Take your hands off the stick. I'm puttin' us down."

And I said to Atta in Arabic: "Next time I'll do the talking. You don't do it very well."

We were now told to go to Venice, even though Jarrah was there – but not to the school where Jarrah was, to another one. There were hundreds of flight schools in Florida, because of the weather there. When storms came over Florida, they were mostly small; there could be flooding on the street where you were, and nothing a block away. In the summertime, the storms moved fast; they rarely hit one area for longer than twenty minutes – unless you got a hurricane, and they were few. So the skies were mostly clear all year – perfect flying conditions. That is why they wanted us in Florida.

This time I did the talking, and it went well. The man we met, who owned the school – a German, I think, from his accent – was not concerned with our instincts, only our finances. The down payment, for the two of us, was ten thousand dollars. I promised to bring the money in within a day or two. As soon as I did, we'd begin.

The German was very friendly, though he didn't ask us anything except for what he needed to know to fill out our applications. Which included our local address. Which we did not have. "Best thing would be to rent a house," the German said. "Until you do, a motel. Wait!" He stuck a finger in the air, and began to wiggle it. "My bookkeeper and his wife, they rent out a spare room. I think the room is empty now. Let me discover this." He grabbed a phone and yelled into it. "Bob! Pick it up!"

"*Ja*," he smiled when he hung up the phone, "the room is available. The price is seventeen dollars a night. That is half the price of the cheapest motel in the area. You will take it, *ja*?"

I turned to look at Atta. He put his hand over his eyes, and with the other, signaled me to walk outside.

Out on the tarmac, Atta was uneasy. "I don't want it. We will have no privacy."

I said: "If we go to a motel, hundreds of people will see us. We will have more privacy in somebody's house."

"They will hear us praying …"

"We will find somewhere else to pray. Or we will make some qadha prayers." Apologetic prayers, for when you have missed the scheduled time. "Anyway, the manual says we can miss some salats, if it is because of other things we are doing for Allah."

Atta had not brought up what was really bothering him – that he was uncomfortable with living so tightly with infidels. He would have to get over that. "It's only a few days," I said, "until we can rent a house."

Finally he nodded. I went back inside alone and told the German the deal was on. He gave me the address of the house, and told me Bob, the bookkeeper, would meet us there after work. Atta was not talkative when we got back to our car.

We stopped first at a branch of the SunTrust Bank. I had noticed this bank's offices wherever we had been in Florida. The banker we talked to, a sloppy man who spilled himself over his desk (and his lunch all over his shirtfront and his cheap ugly tie), was a smiley fellow, eager to please. And, except for a brief pitch of investment opportunities, the opening of a checking account in Atta's name and mine was a mercifully pithy and amiable experience. In Hamburg, they had bitten my head off. I liked Florida.

It was well past the time for lunch, and Atta said he was hungry. We pulled into the parking lot of a Publix supermarket. I followed Atta into the store and to the deli counter. "What can I get you, darlin'?" a countergirl called out.

Atta actually smiled at her. "I am thinking, Ann."

"How do you know her name?" I asked.

"It is written on her shirt."

"Where y'all from?" she asked.

He said: "Saudi Arabia."

"Oh," she bubbled, "I'll bet it is just so *beautiful* there."

He continued to chat with her cheerfully while I puzzled out the reason for this altogether unnatural behavior on his part. She said she had seen the movie *Lawrence of Arabia* and desperately wanted a desert camel ride. He just about promised to get her one, and then the reason came to me. She was African, and a servant, and so not the kind of woman one might think of sexually. And Atta was trying hard to acclimatize. As the manual had instructed us: "When in Rome …"

As we walked from the back of the store to the registers, I suddenly understood that old men and boys who worked for the market were taking the customers' groceries out to their cars, and I saw a sign which advised me that these people were not to be tipped. I marveled at the civility. On a market trip in New Jersey, at the beginning of our drive, the checkout girl had been hard-pressed to spare me a word, or a bag big enough to hold what I had bought after I had nearly been run down by a succession of stone-faced women with carts full of Spaghetti-O's and Count Chocula.

Bob the bookkeeper was, in fact, waiting on his sidewalk. He waved a liver-spotted hand as we pulled up outside his house. Atta was sure he was Jewish, since he was a money professional. But Bob did not look Jewish. He was tall and thin, and feeblish. He wore yellow polyester pants and a similar polo shirt, and he looked like a banana, with his bent back.

The house was small, old, painted white, built of wood close to the sidewalk, separate by only two or three feet from the neighboring homes. The tiny patches of lawn that lined the concrete path to the door were in imminent danger of losing their decorum – but then grass in Florida, a peculiar thick-bladed sort, can grow two inches overnight if the omens are right. I caught a glimpse of a swimming pool in the back. I found later that it was empty, with crinkled brown ficus leaves stuffed in the drains. The plate on the Camry in the driveway read "NOT2NITE." I suspected it belonged to Bob's wife. I also suspected the sentiment was okay with Bob.

There was, as I had guessed there would be, quite a lot of the wife, under the pink quilted sleeping gown she wore when we were introduced in the peach-wallpapered kitchen. She looked us over carefully, as Bob had not, with eyes that were less than welcoming. "Where you fellows from?"

Atta would not answer her, or even acknowledge her presence. I said: "Saudi Arabia." She guffawed.

"Ain't there nobody in your country who don't want to learn how to fly? Jesus, we must get thirty of ya every year." This was no exaggeration, I knew. Most of the men who flew for Saudi airlines had gotten their training in Florida; Saudi military pilots, too. Most Middle Eastern countries train their pilots in the U.S., because it is so much cheaper than anywhere else. There were many of them in the area now, but we were not allowed to contact them, since they were innocent.

"Your room is up on the second floor," she went on. "Turn right at the top of the stairs. Just keep it quiet, huh? Don't bring back no women, like the most of youse do. And don't make no messes I have to clean. You can't use the kitchen, okay? There's a TV in your room, and a set of towels. I'll launder the bedclothes once a week. Bob, show 'em the bathroom. We only got one."

Bob toured us around the house. Then we settled up for one week. When we shut our room's door behind us, Atta pulled the TV plug out of the wall, unpacked his Qur'an, sat down and began to read.

That night I used Atta's cell phone to call the Emirates. A day later our SunTrust account was wired a sum of money – just under ten thousand dollars; the bank would have had to report any larger sum – by a money changer in Sharjah, through Citibank in New York. The day after that, I wrote a check for our flight school tuition. The following morning, our classes began.

The classroom was perhaps half full, twenty people or so, all in the same uniform of sneakers and khaki pants, including several women who might as well have been men. All were perched on the edges of chairs whose arms were desks, like the ones I knew from the classrooms in Germany. There was glee in these people, like children; their legs jittered on their knees and jokes with sexual content were flung around the room. This was to be expected of people learning to fly; but neither Atta nor I could join in it. I found I was excited, yes – but it was a tamped and compressed delight. We sat apart from the others, and kept to ourselves.

All their gusto began to fade when the German approached the blackboard and started scribbling: "Lift and drag vary as

46

the square of the velocity …" I could see eyes squinting, heads being scratched, hard breaths being expelled. But Atta knew what the scribbles meant, and he explained them to me.

Though the school had its own Cockpit Café in a shack on the edge of the tarmac, Atta insisted on lunching each day at the Publix deli counter. It was either a broiled chicken or an Italian submarine. I would have liked to eat elsewhere, but I was always with Atta, and Publix was where he wanted to go. And always bright conversation with the counter girls – but that was all the grace he could muster, and the effort wore him out.

The wife was again in the kitchen when we got home that night, in another pink nightgown and a terrycloth robe. She jumped up quickly and blocked our way to the stairs that led to our room. "You guys splashed water all over the bathroom floor. Don't they have shower curtains where you come from?"

Atta skirted around her, and started up the stairs. Two steps up, he mumbled, without turning around: "It must be nice to sleep all day and do whatever you want."

Steam blew out of the woman's ears. "You little son of a *bitch* …!" Atta continued up the stairs. I turned and shrugged at her.

When Bob came home, she told him to "throw the fuckers out!" He came straight up to our bedroom. "You've been here long enough," he said, "and you need to find a place. I'll give you back your money if you just get out of here." I managed to convince him to let us stay the night. I promised we would go in the morning, and find a house to rent.

When the time came for salat-ul-Isha that night, Atta prayed in his loudest voice (which Allah does not approve), bellowing the rakas and adding extra suras which he recited in English, all of them about infidels roasting in Hell ....

# 6

**Hamburg; Cairo; Dubai: June-August, 1999**

---

The Fat Man pulled up in a Fiat which groaned a sigh of deep relief when his bulk – more than three hundred pounds of it – was transferred to the sidewalk. He patted the car affectionately – he had done auto body work – then moved with surprising agility, a Jackie Gleason mince. He went around to the back of the car, opened the hatchback and lifted out a carton which spilled books and videos onto the street.

After he had huffed up the stairs – Marwan had taken to looking out for him, and had gone down and helped with the box – the Fat Man tore into Atta's store of sweets, which Atta had just replenished. Then, as he did each time he came, he sat down and told Marwan tales. He had gone to Afghanistan, spent time in a training camp, then fought the Afghan Communists with Gulbuddin Hekmatyar. He had joined the jihad in Bosnia, and then, when Sheikh Usama returned to Afghanistan, had

49

gone back to Kandahar and sworn loyalty to the Sheikh. He loved his battle stories; he chuckled over them.

The Fat Man brought Marwan things each time Marwan came to Hamburg, which was happening more and more frequently as the weather warmed and the trees began to flesh themselves out.

Marwan couldn't say why he kept coming back. He hardly ever saw Atta, who was finishing his thesis. Al-Shibh, on the other hand, had too much time for Marwan. He was constantly instructing or questioning, pointing out suras that he wanted Marwan to read, or books by Said Qutb, or shoving Marwan into a chair in front of al-Shibh's computer and bringing up jihadi websites that he insisted Marwan peruse. Even when Marwan was let alone, he kept looking over his shoulder, because al-Shibh might at any moment streak out of his bedroom and call Marwan an idiot. Marwan supposed, in a way, he was flattered that al-Shibh was working on him. But friendship? Warmth? Forget it. Al-Shibh never showed those feelings; he did not know what they were.

But every time Marwan walked into their flat, he felt a throbbing energy, as if he were standing on a compass needle quivering near magnetic north. Al-Shibh and Atta knew what they were intended to do, and all of their thoughts and actions moved them along that path. He did not share that certainty – but he was in awe of it.

Out of respect, he observed their rites – taking his shoes off at their door, performing the ablutions, saying the blessings

Islam requires before or after things. He bought, and wore, a white jalbab, and he grew a beard – not the holy man's face mask, but a circle of hair around his mouth like the Saudi royals wore. He listened to their discussions – because, as al-Shibh said, if you want to make friends with a Muslim man you must understand what he believes, and not expect him to care about what is in your jahili brain.

But when Marwan went back to Bonn, the Muslim dress came off – as did anything he had heard in Hamburg that had threatened to sink in. He returned to his old ways, with one exception: he went to class conscientiously, for a reason he couldn't grasp.

The things the Fat Man brought him when he came to Hamburg were from the back room of At-Tawhid, the Islamic bookshop they all patronized from time to time. Marwan went there himself once or twice, with Atta or al-Shibh. On display in the main room of the store were the usual Muslim volumes, explications of the Qur'an and guides to the proper life: how to pray, what to eat, how to behave yourself. In the back room, where the skulkers went, were the secret things. When they finally let him go in there, he felt the same sort of thrill he felt when he prowled the back rooms of bookstores in Bonn, where they kept the pussy shots.

He read what the Fat Man brought him. Some of it was shit – ravings about Allah and jihad and the glory of martyrdom. But some of it was well thought out, like the speeches he got from al-Shibh, which he had come to appreciate by the time April rolled around. It was easy to agree with al-Shibh that something was terribly wrong. The Muslim world was down and out. That's why Marwan had left it.

Marwan watched the bloody videos not believing his eyes – Chechens dead under Russian tanks. Bosnian mass graves. Palestinians under fire. Big-eyed children in Iraq, starving to death because of the U.N. embargo which America imposed. Flies on the corpses, flies on the kids, maggots crawling in gore … Al-Shibh would dance with fury. "You see what I am telling you? Look what they do to us!" Marwan had heard about these things, but the cameras left out nothing. They probed the wounds, they caught the insects laying their eggs. This was not on TV in Germany. Not shown in Dubai. There was only so much of it you could take. Then, if you were human, something happened to you … you were not the man you had been, self-absorbed and uninvolved.

By June, Atta had finished his thesis, and Marwan had somehow passed his German exam. The future lay before him, but what the hell was it going to be? He would have used the expression "Allah knows," but Marwan did not think Allah had any better idea than Marwan.

"You like computers," Atta said. "Isn't that what you told me? Come to TU Harburg. Electrical engineering. Bahaji is in that program, he can help you pass the entrance exam. And he is getting married soon. Then you can have his room."

Marwan considered the proposition. It made sense. Maybe a little discipline would concentrate his mind, and a concentrated mind might figure out what he ought to do. He thanked Atta profusely for doing the cousinly thing. They agreed that when Bahaji moved out, Marwan would move in.

He spent the summer in Cairo. His mother cried when she saw him. She begged him not to go back. Maybe her moving to Cairo had not been a good idea. She was a widow, forty years old. Her friends from twenty years ago had disappeared into kitchens or buried themselves  under babies and their light under a bushel, as they say. The same thing that she had done.

She would call them and they would be so pleased. She would hear sparks that had been thrown off, years before, from their intellectual fires, from their fascination with literature, from their feet as they had danced for the young men, teasing them with their eyes. But those sparks – an occasional quick laugh, an intelligent joke – floated over dead coals, dropped and died away. So one joke did not lead to another, a laugh was followed not by another laugh but by a sigh. It was finished for them, she realized. They knew it, too. They would not come out to a coffee house. They didn't want to meet.

She had walked, as she had used to walk, to the university. But no one wanted to talk to her – they were all such fledglings: had she ever been that young? And even worse, everything had changed; so many girls were covered up, and she overheard so much anger when she eavesdropped on conversations. So much shouting about Allah, so much hate. Egypt was going to come apart. What was she doing here?

She was lonely. She needed Marwan. But he wouldn't stay. He found Egypt much as she had: desperate. So he had given her three weeks of his time and fled to the emirates – not to Ras al Khaimah, but to Dubai.

Marwan believed – no, he was certain – that Dubai was the best, the most beautiful place in the world. Everything he loved could be found in this tolerant state (more a city, really; outside the capital there was nothing but rock and red sand, except for the gardens where the dates grew on the slopes of the Hajar Mountains). Magnificent white or glass buildings rose along both banks of the Khor Dubai, the "Creek" as they called it, the riverlike incursion of the Arabian Gulf which separated the Deira district from Bur Dubai and ended in a shallow lagoon, home to thousands of flamingos. The buildings – many designed by Arab architects, some of them shaped like the sails of the pearl divers' dhows – were hotels, or the headquarters of corporations that traded throughout the world. You could race along eight-laned Sheikh Zayed Road between towers of glass and steel. If you kept going, you would end up in Abu Dhabi.

But if you walked only a little ways from these sparkling new monuments, you would find yourself in the old town, unchanged from the days when Dubai dhows sailed to India to trade – Bastakiya, on the Khor Dubai, or the area near the Al Fahidi Fort, where the streets were narrow passageways, and square towers with rectangular slits caught the wind to cool the grand houses. Or the separate souks of Deira – the spice souk, the gold souk, the bakeries where flat loaves sent spectacular scents wafting out of tandoor ovens.

He had his monthly student stipend from the Ras al Khaimah government, which hoped, of course, he would use it to learn something useful to Ras al Khaimah. He decided to live as well as he could while he was in Dubai. He rented a red BMW Z3 and drove it to the luxury Jumeirah Beach Hotel, a six-hundred room facility shaped like a breaking wave. He had never seen anything like the room they let him into, more than fifty square metres of glass, rich textile and stone.

He lay in a hot Jacuzzi for an hour or so; then, as the sun set in front of him, he walked along the sand, then had his car brought out to him and drove from hotel to hotel, from bar to pub to disco, until he found what he was looking for. She was British, and she was horny, and she loved his room – although between bouts of frenetic sex, she would climb out of bed and wonder, aloud, what it might be like to fuck at the Burj al Arab, which she had been told was the most extravagant hotel in the world, and which she could see out Marwan's window, just across the beach.

He dumped her back where he had found her, and drove through town alone, his eyes glued to the white Grand Mosque, all lit up in the night, with its high, thin minarets erect, as he had been. He could have gone on to Sharjah, the neighboring emirate, and even to Ras al Khaimah. But he decided he would rather not.

He spent about a month in Dubai. For the first week, he passed lazy days, letting the sun bake the German weather out of his bones; and every night was like the one before, except that the girls were different – no, really, they were the same. In the second week, he left the hotel – he could not afford any more of it – and found a less expensive room in the business section of Deira. He went from tower to tower, studying their directories, trying to determine from non-committal names what a company's business was, and whether it intrigued him. But nothing was captivating – and even if something had been, he had no skills, no references, he didn't know anyone, he knew they would not hire him so he didn't even ask.

For the third and fourth weeks, he did nothing. Then he turned in the BMW and went back to Germany.

When he returned to Hamburg in August, he knew something had changed. There was no greeting when Atta met him at the door. Atta motioned him in, then turned away and walked to the table where al-Shibh and the Fat Man sat with their hands folded in front of them, looking to Marwan as he imagined a panel of judges would look. Atta sat beside them and adopted the same pose. I must have made a mistake, Marwan thought. But what could it possibly be?

Atta said: "Sit down, Marwan."

"Okay," said Marwan. "What's up?"

"They are fighting again in Chechnya. Al-Shibh and I want to go."

Marwan breathed a sigh of relief. But that was for him, not for them. For some time, he had sensed they were making plans. But this plan seemed foolish to him. "You'll get murdered," he told Atta. "You don't know how to fight."

"Marwan, you have completely forgotten where I have been."

"I don't think you should do this …"

"We are going to go to Afghanistan to see Sheikh Usama. He will help us sneak into Chechnya. We think you should come along."

"Me?" Marwan said, shaking his head. "I don't think so."

"Okay, so you don't want to fight," the Fat Man interrupted, turning his huge hands dangerously loose. "You should go with them anyway. Maybe they will find something else for you to do."

"I have to think about going to school …"

"Do that later," al-Shibh said. "What do you care about school?"

And al-Shibh was right, Marwan realized. He didn't care about school. He didn't care about anything – except these men, who were trying to help him (in their own peculiar way); who were looking out for him, with whom he felt as at home as he had at any time in his life. Now they were going to leave him – and he did not want to be left.

"Okay, I'll go with you."

"Good," Atta said.

# 7

**Venice, Florida: August, 2000**

---

Atta insisted I back-seat his training flights, but he would not come on mine. It betokened a certain lack of faith, which I resented after a time.

We learned the four fundamentals – turns, climbs, descents and straight and level; the three axes of rotation – pitch, roll and yaw; how to use the elevators, the ailerons, the rudder pedals, and why, and when; rolled into turns and out of them at thirty degrees of bank, then at ninety; and the most important thing – that on the straight and level the plane is stable *if you leave it alone*. It took Atta two lessons for that to sink in. I had already learned it on our flight in Sarasota, when Atta had tried to get us killed ahead of time.

The school had a computer room, which we used every day – Atta to get instructions, I to make sure that money kept coming to our account. The room was off the classroom, behind a set of folding doors. There was no way to lock the doors, and students were constantly coming in to practice the theory exam, giving us that pissed-off look when we stayed on the keyboards too long. Bahaji had taught us how to use twenty digit encryption, but the school's computers hadn't the speed or the software to handle it. We were forced to use open code; we were exposed and vulnerable, not just to people wandering in but to people watching the emails. But if anyone was watching, they did not draw conclusions.

We had moved out of Bob the bookkeeper's and rented a two-bedroom pink stucco house five miles from the airport in Nakomis Beach. Used it to study, pray and sleep. Did not order cable. Filled the kitchen cabinets with Twinkies and Oreos.

I don't know if Atta knew how to cook, but he wouldn't, and I couldn't, so we ate out every night. In Hamburg, if we had eaten in, al-Shibh had prepared the meal. I missed his Yemeni cuisine: rice, meat and vegetables, all of it spiced with hawayil, a mix of hot Indian seasonings.

A beautiful woman lived next door. She looked like Sharon Stone. She walked a puppy every day, in the late afternoon. At first, she had shown a dazzling smile when we passed her by; but that disappeared when Atta ignored her and made me do the same. In the end she turned sullen and nasty, shrieking when Atta poked at the dog on a rainy day with his umbrella. Poor woman – she did not understand that the Prophet forbids us to keep a dog, unless for hunting or guarding. On top of that, it was a black dog, which the Prophet has said is a devil and must be killed.

We spoke to no one. It was a lonely time. Late on the nights of the full moon, I barefooted the bright white beach, sand liquid like mercury between my toes, thinking of how lovely the world would be if Americans had only learned to mind their own damned business.

Atta would burn off tension with aimless drives through the Venice streets, going nowhere in particular, looking at nothing much. But on one of those drives he jammed on his brakes and pointed to our left. There I saw a public park. A basketball game was going on, and Ziad Jarrah was playing in it.

I started to get out of the car, but Atta pulled me back. He honked the horn; everyone stared, and Jarrah recognized him.

"How's flying?" Jarrah grinned as he climbed into our back seat.

Atta turned to look at him. "What are you doing?"

"I can sink three pointers," Jarrah laughed.

"Allah does not care about basketball."

"Tell that to Kareem Abdul Jabbar."

"Stick to your business, Jarrah!"

Jarrah's grin grew wider still. "I've finished the private pilot course. The business is well in hand." Then the fun slipped off his face. "Have you heard about al-Shibh?"

Atta nodded. "It is not good."

"What about him?" I asked. Atta never told me anything.

Jarrah answered me. "They will not give him a visa to come to the U.S."

"Why not? We had no trouble."

"He has tried twice. He says it's because he is a Yemeni. Yemenis have a history of overstaying their visas. They don't want to give him the opportunity."

Atta was extremely perturbed. "What is he doing about it?"

"He's going to go to Yemen, try it again from there. Maybe catch someone asleep."

"He must get into this country!"

"Don't worry, he will."

"I told him to get false papers! Try another name! Why is he not thinking?"

"He's doing the best he can!"

On the playground, they were calling for Jarrah, more and more obscenely. Jarrah shrugged and kicked the car door open. "I'm going to a wedding in Lebanon. I'll see if I can help."

"You have no time to go to a wedding!"

Jarrah climbed out and banged the door shut. "Excuse me! I still have a life. And just for your information, the people who will be at this wedding are very westernized. Including my parents, just so you know. Some of them will be Christians. Friends of mine. My girlfriend is going, too. *We* might get married. If we don't, we are going to get seriously drunk and boogie all night long."

After Jarrah stormed off, Atta hunched grimly over the wheel, and we rolled down the streets of Venice at twenty-five miles an hour until it was nearly midnight and I had fallen asleep.

I had noticed that in America the surest way to draw attention to yourself is to shut other people out. The rest of the world will respect your desire to be let alone; but Americans cannot tolerate other people's privacy. They believe it is a sickness not to relate – not just to people who interest them, but to everyone – and they are gravely offended if they are not at once allowed into everyone's innermost heart.

They abhor silence. It terrifies them. It makes them confront their emptiness. So they never stop talking, so they don't have to think. They talk about sports, or celebrities, or each other's little lives – and if they run out of things to say, they turn on the television and let the professionals do it.

Atta could not open up, but I could. I did not court my classmates, but I relaxed my lips from their constant frown and let my eyes loose to wander the room and, possibly, be caught.

One of the mannish ladies sauntered up to me one day at break. Her hair was cut short, with short bangs; she wore khakis and sneakers and a polo shirt embroidered with the flying school's logo. She said: "Can I ask you something?"

"Sure. Why not?"

She cocked her head to one side, and placed an arm akimbo. "Why is it, when it's so damn hot, your friend is always so buttoned up? I mean, long pants, long sleeve shirt – what's that about? And why is it that when he flies you always go up with him? I mean, nobody else has a passenger. I mean, how come?"

"That's *two* somethings," I scolded her.

"Well, jeez, pal, regrets!"

"I will tell you," I whispered, "but you must promise me you will tell no one what I say. Do you promise?" Of course she did. Her head cocked to the other side to make room for new information. "He is not my friend. He is a Saudi prince. I am his bodyguard."

"Damn!" she squealed. "I knew it!" Then she put on a conspiratorial look, and whispered *her* secret to me. "I've always wanted to go to Saudi Arabia."

And she would do anything to get there. That is what she was telling me.

"I don't think you would like it."

"Is it true they won't let a woman drive a car?"

"Yes, it's true. You shouldn't go."

A little storm blew through her eyes. "I'm going to fly for the Air Force. So maybe I just will."

I didn't think so. "By the time you can fly an F-16, there will be no American air base in Saudi Arabia."

"Maybe," she admitted. Then dawned a smile. "How

about lunch at the Cockpit Café?"

I shook my head regretfully. "Oh, I'm sorry, but we Saudis can only eat kosher food."

"What? I thought you-all hated the Jews."

"That is because we have to eat their food. Have you ever had gefilte fish? Oh, my God!"

Of course she revealed the secret to everyone in the class. From then on, though Atta did not change, they were respectful to him. Okay, he was arrogant – but he had a right to be.

As we walked into the flying school's office, the receptionist waved at me. "Your friend's got an email from his girlfriend in Germany."

"Your girlfriend?" I chuckled to Atta. "That will be the day."

"Don't be crude. Anyway, I had a girlfriend once."

"You did? I don't believe you."

"Don't ever call me a liar. I don't lie."

"All right, then," I smiled. "Who was she?"

"And don't ask me personal questions. Let's go read the mail."

The email turned out to be from al-Shibh. He had been in Yemen, he told us in code – had seen Jarrah there. Had applied again for a visa, and had wired money to Jarrah, who was back in Florida, to enroll him at the flight school where Jarrah himself was training. He hoped to be with his boyfriend soon. He had signed it "Jenny, with lots of love."

65

On a bright blue Florida day, I took off alone. Without the instructor's added weight, the plane jumped into the sky. The water below me was flat all the way to Mexico. I put the plane through every maneuver I had learned. I was afraid of nothing. It was beautiful!

"*Allah-hu akhbar*!" Jenny's next email crowed. God is great! "And keep your ears open for something very good!"

# 8

**Peshawar: November, 1999**

---

The taxi followed the Khyber Road into new Peshawar, the Saddar or Cantonment area on the west of the city, which the British, when they had occupied Pakistan (it was part of India then) had built to keep away the filthy little wogs. It was all wide avenues edged with tall trees, their trunks painted white, and big one-story houses with huge, well-groomed lawns. Marwan could smell roses as he stuck his head out the window for a better look. But this was not the Peshawar he was meant to see.

Atta, al-Shibh and Marwan were each traveling alone. Marwan had been told to go to Peshawar and find the Honey Man. The cab driver knew where the Honey Man was. They were going to him now.

The taxi turned right on the Hospital Road and passed the U.S. Consulate. The driver opened his window and spat as they passed it by. Left on the Mall Road past the Deans Hotel; right on to the Railway Road and across the tracks of the Cantt, the British railroad which used to run to the Khyber Pass. And there was the old city ahead of them.

They turned into the Qissa Khwani Bazaar, the Street of the Storytellers. The road was narrow and packed to the curbs with pushcarts, horse carts, donkey carts, bikes, manpowered wagons. Three-wheeled minicabs built on blue motor scooters fought for a path with SUVs and twelve-ton trucks, most of them unmuffled and sending up an ear-splitting racket as they banged against each other and scattered pedestrians.

On either side were buildings three stories high, the lower floors filled with awninged selling stalls, the second with Marwan didn't know what behind wooden balustrades of Moorish arches. The third had smaller balustrades; they were unroofed and unused, as if they had been burned out a hundred years ago. Huge Coca Cola signs were everywhere. So were Pakistani troops, in helmets and battle gear, clustered around their armored cars parked at the intersections. They were there, the driver told him in Farsical Arabic, because: "Army make coup one month ago, arrest the government. Also somebody shooting rockets at Americans in Karachi."

The teashops, with big brass samovars, and china teapots and tea bowls hanging from the walls, were crowded with men – Afghans, Iranis, Uzbeks, Tajiks, Pathans – enjoying their last hookahs before they went off to pray. Behind these shops was the labyrinth, the unmarked streets of the souk. There the buildings stretched up to four, five or six stories high and leaned toward each other over increasingly slender alleys of stone and ancient brick. Marwan thought Atta would have loved these streets with their tawny-colored walls, the upper stories decorated with wood in geometric designs and overhanging the ground floor like an overbite. But he would not have loved the songs that curled up from a hundred cassettes out a hundred windows as the sun began to set.

On the Cloth Street, the Bird Street, the Fruit and Honey Streets, the Street for Brains, the Street for Livers, the Streets of Rugs and Guns, the Video Street, the Inkjet Street, the Street for Tourist Junk, metal shutters slammed down as the muezzins sent out the adhan standing in minarets, not on a pre-recorded tape as had become the practice in so many other towns. That had happened in Ras al Khaimah, and Marwan was convinced that it had broken his father's heart. It had killed his father, he thought.

From there, Marwan lost track of directions, but the streets became more constricted and shabby and decayed. They passed a cemetery. He could see, through a gate in the wall, a yard paved with tile in which tinsel hung from the trees, out of which came the agreeable smell of nag champa and sandalwood. Beggars sat at the entranceway with wooden begging bowls. And across from there was another space where there must have been a hundred men, all Marwan's age, sitting four or five to a bamboo mat, passing the chillum, the hookah. The scent from there was not incense. He tapped the driver's shoulder. "What is that smell?"

"Hashish. Or heroin."

"Is it legal here?"

"No. But it is not alcohol, and the police they leave you alone for fifty rupees in the hand. You get ten grams of that tirra for twenty-five rupees. The Taliban, they smuggle it in from Afghanistan. But only for unbelievers. No Muslim should fool with that." The driver turned his head, and looked where Marwan was looking. "But these men, it is not their fault – they are desperate."

No work without a bribe, he explained; no money to bribe without work. Trained engineers, and four-year-old kids, filled horseback pallets with fresh-kilned bricks in the clay pits of Dabaray Ghara.

Now they entered a rotting street of blue facades filled with cinemas and cinema ads, huge billboards of underdressed Bollywood stars, nailed to the second stories. The businesses here were wretched: hitting car engines with sledges to break them up for scrap; gouging intestines out of goats for bad-smelling leather. Men rode on the roofs of the buses to get to the mosque on time. The beggars here were disgusting, leprous and dismembered. As the sun sank down, Marwan heard gunshots coming from hidden courtyards.

You look out the window, he thought, and all you see at first are all the beautiful colors, the exotic hats and faces … it is a picture that excites you, you think of it as rich. Then you get stuck in a traffic jam, things don't go by so fast, you get a longer look at them and after a while you realize that the exotic faces are worn down, the vivid costumes are threadbare – that you are in a filthy, backward place, a place where no one should have to live in this century.

What if you had not been so lucky, he thought? What if you had not been born in the desert, on the sea? What if you were out there, struggling in these streets, at best living by your wits, at worst a beast of burden, hopeless and condemned?

How had so many of us ended up like this? Or been unable to rise above it? And there but for – what? Indiscriminate fate? – could go I … Maybe these were the worst of us – maybe not even the worst – but we were all sinking on this boat, on one deck or another.

We who invented paper and the hospital, algebra and the zephirum, the concept of the zero, were now dirt in the eye of the world which managed to care about some of us only because we walked on top of a black ooze the world could not do without. Al-Shibh has it right. We are contemptible.

He closed his eyes tight, not to see what he had seen. And then he found it hard to breathe, and he felt like he needed to weep. He had not cried for a long, long time. He had not cried for his father. The last time he had felt tears welling up was when his father had whipped him – he was a little boy – for some infraction he was guilty of, which he could not remember now.

The taxi stopped before an anonymous old building, also blue. He paid the driver and ambled into what, from its rows of chairs and blackboards, was obviously a madrassa, and through it into another room with a curtain for a door. The room smelled fresh and was spotlessly clean, not like the world outside. A man with glasses over an eye patch, and a white djellaba and turban, sat cross-legged on a rug on the floor, the only furnishing. He seemed tall, and very thin – but Marwan had the sense that under his robe he was a massive man, that he was a butcher knife masquerading as a stiletto.

"Are you the Honey Man?" Marwan asked. The man nodded that he was. "I am …" Marwan began to explain.

"Yes, I can see who you are. How was your journey?"

"Long."

"Then you must be hungry." The Honey Man reached behind him and brought out a plate of ground beef on a flat round piece of unleavened bread. "Chappli kebab," he chuckled. "Tomatoes, green chilis and eggs. A Peshawar specialty." He reached behind him once again and brought out a pot of green tea. "Relax a while. Have the food. Then we will talk. Sorry, there are no utensils."

Marwan had not realized how hungry he was. The chappli was hot and spicy, and the tea perked him up. It took him no more than two minutes to finish all of it, the Honey Man all the while smiling and nodding his head.

When Marwan had wiped his plate clean, the Honey Man reached out and took it and put it behind him again. "Now," he said, "I understand that you are an unbeliever."

Marwan thought about it. Was he an unbeliever? No, he didn't think so. "I am not an unbeliever," he said. "I just don't care."

"What do you mean, you 'don't care'?"

Marwan had once loved God greatly, as his father had taught him to – until God had failed to punish him for what he was doing under the bushes. That puzzled Marwan – he pushed God further, and still he found himself untouched. Marwan began to conclude that either God was busy with more significant sin, or He did not care what happened to anyone or what anybody did. He remembered the Saudi princes who obeyed Allah at home, then broke all of His commandments in London or New York. *There* was significant sin, and corruption on top of it. Yet Marwan knew of no way in which God had chastised *them*. He thought of his God-fearing father and his miserable end. He had never been rewarded for his piety – unless it was in Paradise, and that, to Marwan, was too little and far too late. And what of all the suffering in the Fat Man's video tapes? He thought: if Allah sits in Paradise uninterested in us, then why should I be interested in Him? "Emir," he said, "I just don't think it matters what we believe. Maybe Allah made the world, but He is not running it now."

"Then you are an unbeliever," the Honey Man scowled, "because you are ungrateful to Allah. '*Surely, those who are too arrogant to worship Me will enter Gehenna, forcibly.*' You know that verse?" Marwan nodded. "Then are you not afraid?"

"If I am wrong, Allah will show me …"

The Honey Man threw up his hands. "Oh no no no! You misunderstand. Allah will show you nothing. You must find your faith alone."

Marwan shrugged. "But I am not looking for it."

"Ah," said the Honey Man, squinting. "I should send you home. But your cousin has asked me to see you. So I want to ask you: why are you here?"

"Because my friends were coming, and they suggested that I come …"

The Honey Man tapped a finger on the floor between his knees. "You fly half the way around the world because someone suggested it? No one is that aimless. I know what you are doing here. Why don't you?"

"I don't know what you think …" Marwan said. But he did know, and he had to turn away, because – against his wishes – he was crying again.

"You are here because you have no idea what to do with yourself."

How pathetic – it's that obvious, Marwan thought. Maybe they were really the lucky ones, the people in the streets of Peshawar he was feeling so badly for, the people who had no choices – who only had time to think about how they were going to feed themselves, and when, where and whether they were going to get some sleep.

And then … he had one of those moments. The kind of moment you have when you're young, and then only once or twice. Out of all the numbered lottery balls tumbling in the barrel, the right ones popped up the tube; his longings had an order, and things came clear. "I could do something for them … those people … I could help …"

"What people?"

"The people out there." Out the doorway. The people in the alleyways. The people on top of the buses.

"Really? You want to help them?" The Honey Man waggled a finger. "But you do not want to make jihad. Do I understand correctly? You will not pick up a weapon."

"No. I couldn't do that." Marwan was certain on that point. He couldn't stomach violence. The Fat Man's videos had made him puke.

"So what kind of help are we talking about?"

Marwan thought, but the vision went just so far. "They said you would tell me that."

"Your cousin thinks I am a genius," the Honey Man laughed. "But what can I do with you? You have no skills, no talents. It is ridiculous. You want to help these people – but these people are Muslims, and you have little faith. You can do nothing for them. They do not want help from you.

"Those who come to see me come for Allah's sake. They will do what He commands them to – and I tell them what that is. But you want to choose what you will do – and that

75

you will never accomplish, because you have a serious problem: you do not know who you are."

Now that busy finger was stiff and straight and pointed at Marwan's nose. "*You* are the one who needs the help. And these tears I see, they are for yourself, not for 'the people out there.'"

Marwan became quickly angry. If he finally knew what he wanted, who was this emir to say that he was wrong? And how could it not be clear to the man that these people needed all the help they could get, from wherever they could get it?

"Understand," the emir said quickly. "I do not mean to offend you."

Marwan was not much offended, though. He was disappointed. More than that, he was fed up, with himself and everything. "Thank you for your time, emir. I think I should go home."

"No." The Honey Man held up a hand. "I do not give up on you. You have to think this through, my friend. And in that I will assist you, because your cousin asked me to." He rose and walked toward the doorway. "Come. Let's take a ride."

They drove in his black Land Cruiser to the good part of Peshawar. The House of Martyrs was a compound, a British house from the time of the Raj, part Tudor, part Victorian, behind a lawn and a wall. On the roof was a round tower, with a Queen Anne peak. Somebody was in it. Something glinted in the sun.

The driveway gates swung open. The Honey Man drove in. "You will sleep here tonight," he said. "We will send you out tomorrow."

# 9

**Venice, Florida: October, 2000**

---

It was the end of the hurricane season. There had been no significant storms.

Atta had been difficult; the instructor did not like him. But he had advanced so quickly that he had been allowed to take up the Seneca, the school's only twin-prop plane, before he had even begun the work toward the multi-engine rating. I was not moving quite so fast; I was still working on IFR, the instrument flight rating, which is what John-John Kennedy should have done before he flew to Martha's Vineyard in a disorienting fog.

We were sitting in T.G.I. Friday's, getting the Early Bird Special. The restaurant had a TV on, showing a sitcom to two women alone at the bar, and the two of us. I had just ordered a hamburger when the sitcom disappeared; ABC posted "Breaking News," and there was Peter Jennings with papers in his hand. Something big was happening besides the coming election.

"Six U.S. sailors are dead, thirty-six injured and eleven missing after two terrorists on a suicide mission attacked a U.S. Navy destroyer today in the Middle Eastern port city of Aden."

The picture shifted; we saw a ship with a massive hole in the port side amidships. The edges of the hole were sharp and ragged like the opened lid of a tuna fish can.

"U.S. officials said an explosion occurred when a small boat assisting in the refueling of the U.S.S. Cole pulled alongside the destroyer. Two individuals on board the small boat were helping to gather up the mooring lines of the Cole, officials said."

Small boats cruised by the destroyer. Harbormen, not terrorists. After the fact.

"The individuals took one line out to an anchor buoy and were coming back for a second line when the explosion tore a twenty-foot by forty-foot gash in the mid-hull section at around 12:15 local time, or 5:15 a.m. Eastern."

Atta gaped at the screen.

"The blast was strong enough to blow out windows hundreds of yards away. The damage was concentrated in one of the engine rooms, and flooding has been controlled."

Here was Jennings again, well-coifed.

"The incident may be linked to alleged terrorist

mastermind Osama bin Laden, U.S. officials have told ABC News."

Sheikh Usama was kneeling, looking down the barrel of an AK-47.

"Although U.S. intelligence sources have no specific information that bin Laden is responsible, they say he could be a suspect because his is one of the few groups capable of such an attack."

Sheikh Usama walking with other people I did not recognize.

"The perpetrators must have had knowledge of the few hours the ship would be in port and the ability to infiltrate the harbor at that time, the ability to assemble strong explosives on the small boat, and they also had to know what part of the ship to target. Bin Laden is said to have strong ties to Yemen, as his father came from that country."

Sheikh Usama cross-legged on the floor. Two Taliban mullahs and a dented teapot.

"Intelligence sources tell ABC News that six days ago, the United States received information that bin Laden signaled one of his hit squads to 'move out,' but there were no details on where it was headed."

Atta leapt to his feet and ran out of the restaurant. I picked up the wallet he had left behind and scrambled to catch up.

"That is what al-Shibh was talking about! They pulled it off!" He was trying to keep his voice down, and dragging me to our car. "You drive, Marwan! Get me home! Before I show these infidels something they should not see!"

I beeped the doors on the driver's side and slid behind the wheel. "Atta, did you know about this?"

He bounced into the passenger seat. "Yes! But I did not know when! Drive fast, Marwan! I have rejoicing to do!"

# 10

**Kandahar: November, 1999**

They woke Marwan out of a beautiful dream: three women under the hijab, the head covering, coming to him from far away over undulating fields of grass scythed a foot high.

Laid out on the bed were a black turban and a black jalbab. When a mujihad came to get Marwan, he unwrapped the turban Marwan had already put on without knowing how to do it, and rewrapped it over Marwan's face, hiding all but his eyes. Marwan followed him down narrow wooden stairs, and came out of the house at the back. The black Toyota was waiting there; another mujihad behind the wheel was tapping his wrists on the ring. Marwan was ushered into the back seat, and the truck sped out of the compound gate and drove beyond Peshawar's western edge through the huge Kachagari Refugee Camp and the Kharkhanai Bazaar, up into the foothills of the Khyber Pass.

Christ went to the desert to find himself. Mohammad did the same. There is something in desolate terrain which sets the soul aflight. Americans, Marwan mused, go to their national parks. They might as well go to Disney World. But they do not like desolation, unless it is fully equipped.

The road was brown, the mountains were brown, the air was brown with the dust they flung as they raced up the switchbacks toward the Afghan border. Tiny walled forts were everywhere, the homes of Afridi tribesmen, with mud walls twenty-five feet high, metal gates and watchtowers. Everyone Marwan saw had an AK-47 slung over a shoulder. No one trusted anyone. Hadn't for centuries.

The black Toyota lurched to a stop. "Get out," said the driver. "Walk."

"But …"

"You find over there a dry riverbed. You follow it." The driver reached back and opened the door Marwan was sitting next to, then gave him a fairly gentle shove – not an order, more a hint. Marwan tumbled out of the SUV; the driver backed, turned around and left him standing there.

Marwan climbed to the top of a little hill, keeping his head down. From there he could see a mud hut, and several soldiers slumped beside it. It was the checkpoint on the border of the Northwest Frontier Provinces, where nobody but the local clan chiefs had any say. This was the most dangerous of boundaries – or, as the driver had warned him, "Don't let the tribals catch you. They fuck you up the ass."

Sliding back down the hill, Marwan found the riverbed the driver had told him about. Every step he took along it clattered, as stones worn smooth when the freshets ran shifted under his feet. When he had gone about a hundred metres – the distance he estimated it was to the border post – he dropped on his stomach and crawled. Two hundred metres further on, a road crossed the riverbed. It was out of view of the border post because of a higher hill, and he chose to get off his belly and walk along it. He had no map and no idea where he was to go. But after he had walked two miles, an ochre cloud announced the approach of a white Toyota pickup with a shiny chrome rollbar and black tinted windows. It skidded to a stop beside him. The driver, another mujihad, waved: "Get in."

They drove by green fields along the Kabul River, and then past the Bab-e-Khyber watchtower and under the arch at Jamrud Fort and into the rocky waistline of the Khyber Pass. The old British Khyber railway tracks ran in and out of view. The pass was not as forbidding as the British would have one believe, but mountains pitched down to both sides of the road's hairpin curves, and at Ali Masjid, where British died, the width of the pass was no more than sixteen metres or so. Ambush would have been simple almost anywhere.

They drove on through the smugglers' bazaar at Landi Kotal. At Torkham, the Afghani border post with its great black iron gates, the road was edged with mud hut shops, their owners napping on stretchers the Russians had left behind, and hawala bankers showed their cash in glass display cases. The gateway was jammed with buses, trucks, all filled to the roofs (and on the roofs) with Afghans and Pakistanis, and hundreds more on the sides of the road wheelbarrowing everything they owned either into or out of Afghanistan. But the mujihad was Taliban. The crossing was no sweat. The Pakis supported the Taliban. And they wanted Marwan to go – to get the hell out of Pakistan before he disrupted things there.

They dropped into the Nangahar valley, the road here lined with poplar trees and what was left of the summer's crop, the pink and white fields of opium poppy. An itchy-fingered klatch of Taliban stopped them at Bhati Kot, asking for the password. Thank God the driver had it – of course, Marwan smiled, he *would*. They searched everything anyway, just for the heck of it.

A ways on, scattered firs and cypresses announced Jalalabad – or what was left of it - there seemed to be no roofs. Past there, the Toyota ran once again along the Kabul River. Stone Buddhas sat in the cliff caves on the other bank. At the Darunta Reservoir, music the Taliban forbade rang out of the tea houses, and here and there an uncovered woman gleaned the fields.

But from there as far as Sarobi, the road was no more than a goat path. It had been good at one time, the driver said, but rough combat with the Russians – and, after that, with the warlords, until the Taliban beat Massoud there and Kabul fell – had devastated the asphalt, tank treads and mortars chewing it up, the worst as the road wound through Tangi Abreshom. Blown-up armor was everywhere – the Taliban had no equipment to search out mines, so they just drove over them and got through if Allah willed it. Now geezers and kids pitched dirt into a hundred thousand potholes, running to catch the cash the drivers tossed out the window at them.

Then past the Naglu Reservoir and through Tangi Gharu gorge. After nine hours of driving, the last of it again through steeply climbing switchbacks and hairpin turns, they rolled into Kabul. Marwan spent the night, dog-tired and cold, in a house in Zarnegar, close to the Pul-e-Khisti – the bridge of bricks – and the blue-domed mosque of the same name where he was brought for salat-ul-Isha. Most of Kabul was rubble left by the battles between the warlords. In the very early morning, they were off again.

It was five hundred kilometers from Kabul to Kandahar – fourteen hours of driving over brutal stones and heaves like the sea in a typhoon. "If you come from Quetta," the driver said, "it is a much shorter trip. The other ones go through Quetta. But this is the way I was told to go. So I go."

There were times when he took the truck off-road, which was an easier ride. Half of the bridges were bombed out and the traffic that kept to what once had been a major thoroughfare delighted in playing chicken with any vehicle that approached, firing off Kalashnikovs when a coward swerved away. The temperature rose as they drove southwest by a welcome ten degrees. They passed by Ghazni and Qalat-e-Ghilzai through brown countryside, sharp mountains off away, Marwan could not tell how far. The dirt rose and blinded them for the road ahead, until an increasing herd of villagers, pushing goats and sheep, announced the outskirts of Kandahar.

They delivered him to a house they called al-Ghumad, deep in the city, on an unnamed street. On the roof was a satellite dish. Inside was a busy office. A large map of the world hung on one of its walls; brochures and pamphlets and documents were piled on folding tables, and laptops were everywhere. Mujahidin were working here. They paid no attention to Marwan. He heard no Pashtun or Farsi, only Arabic.

He was led up to the second floor, to a room about the size of the bedrooms in Atta's flat, and similarly furnished – bed, desk, chair. The mujihad pushed him in and shut the door behind him. He heard a key turn in the lock.

They left him alone for two hours. That was not a good idea, because all he could think about during that time was: What am I doing here? And if it turns out I don't like this place, how do I get out?

Then the mujihad returned for him. He moved Marwan roughly back down the stairs and into what was obviously a small lecture hall. On the back wall there was a blackboard; in front of it, a table with deep gouges cut into it, scattered with books and papers; and in front of that a number of the usual classroom chairs. The mujihad stood behind the table, and motioned for Marwan to sit. He stared at Marwan a moment; then he barked: "Iqra! The Cow!"

He was ordering Marwan to recite the second sura of the Qur'an. Marwan was happy he remembered it. He did not want to make the man mad.

"'*Bi ism 'Allah ar-Rah'man ar-Rah'im. Alef Lam Mim. That is the Book, wherein is no doubt, a guidance to the godfearing …*'"

"Is that you?" the mujihad shouted. "The godfearing? No! Go on."

"' *… As for the unbelievers, alike it is to them whether thou hast warned them or hast not warned them, they do not believe …*'"

"Is *that* you? Go on!"

"' *… And some men there are who say, 'We believe in God and the Last Day'; but they are not believers …*'"

"Is *that* you? You must be one of the three!! Go on."

"' *… In their hearts is a sickness, and God has increased their sickness …*'"

The questioner picked up a book and slammed it down. "*That* is you! Go on."

"' *… And there awaits them a painful chastisement …*'"

The book came up and slammed down again. "Are you warned, jahili?"

"I … "

"Don't talk! Listen! We already know what you have to say!" The mujihad sat on the desk, half turned away from Marwan. "You love your Muslim brothers? Is that what you want us to believe? Well – we do not believe it. You are full of shit. If the Qur'an does not guide your life … then who are you to us?"

He turned full on to Marwan, who saw in his expression what he had seen in al-Shibh's. "And you would do what we do? Do you know what that is? *'This is the recompense of those who fight against God and His Messenger, and hasten about the earth, to do corruption there: they shall be slaughtered, or crucified, or their hands and feet shall alternately be struck off, or they shall be banished from the land …'"*

He carefully picked up another book and pointed it at Marwan. "You will read this Qur'an from this moment until you are half blind! And then you will come here and repeat it. *'We shall make thee recite, to forget not what God wills'*!"

For days, they would not let him sleep. Ten minutes for food, fifteen minutes of rest, two hours of reading in the room they had locked him into, then two or three hours of this lecturing, as one or another mujihad paced back and forth behind the desk.

They read the Qur'an. He recited it. And maybe it was because he was tired, or maybe he was changing, but the splendorous sound of its syllables – as they had when he was a child – began to spill passion over each other, until he wanted to cry. They showed him more bloody videos, and tapes of scholars pronouncing fatwas that authorized attacks against Jews and Americans. Video wills left behind by Palestinian suicide bombers. Death, and determination, that is what he saw and heard.

He didn't know if he could have walked out if he had wanted to. Either he was a prisoner, or they were locking him in because there were things they did not want him to see. But it didn't matter – he was not ready to leave. As much as they were watching him, he was watching them – the mujahidin who harangued him, the people who passed him on the stairs as he was moved from place to place. He had had glimpses of other rooms, full of computers and phones. It all began to enchant him. Not so much what they told him – he had heard much of that before. But their organization, their decisiveness, so un-Arabic. He could tell from the accents he heard that there were men working in this house from all over the Arab world, all of them treated as equals. Where else was that going on? Nowhere, as far as he knew. He admired all that. He respected it. Although they never spoke about building things, only about destroying them.

By the third day, though, he was exhausted. His mind seemed to be wandering, and he was not sure they actually said what he thought they said. He thought they had moved from politics to medieval tales, and he was in the state of mind to be plied with that sort of thing. He remembered one of them saying America served the Dajjal – the one-eyed Devil, the Deceiver from the ancient Arabian texts. But there would soon come a Mahdi, the man said, a Messiah, the true khalifa, and the Mahdi would slaughter America and conquer the Western world. And then would come the final war, the Armageddon, when the Dajjal fought against Islam with his army of Masons and Jews and the Children of Fornication, who were numerous in the West. But the Mahdi would wipe out this army with germs and hydrogen bombs. Then the world would convert to Islam, and peace would envelope all.

By the fifth day, he was not listening, he could not work his brain; but the mujihad was working it without his help. He was telling Marwan what the Qur'an said about the martyr's reward. "From the moment the first drop of your blood is spilled, you do not feel the pain of your wounds, you are forgiven for all your sins; you see your seat in Paradise, you are saved from the horror of Judgment Day; you gain the crown of honor, the least precious stone of which is better than this entire world. The black-eyed await you in Paradise, as pure as pearls in oysters, whom no hand has touched, to whom no dirt adheres. They will await you in your pavilions, to pleasure you. Seventy-two. Imagine it! Such endless, exquisite joy!"

And suddenly Marwan saw them – not all seventy-two, just three or four – gliding on a marble floor, in and out of archways, white-robed and shining, with big full breasts, the whites of their eyes gleaming, the pupils like obsidian, lips pomegranate-red, the robes dropping down off their shoulders, their nipples erect, their pelvises undulating, submission in the eyes ... "*What do you want?*" they said ...

He put his hand inside his pants. The mujihad yanked it out. "You are not in Paradise yet," he scowled. "You wait here."

# 11

## Venice, Florida: December, 2000

---

Angels like winged Cabbage Patch dolls hung from Venice's lampposts holding electric candles, half of the bulbs burnt out. Christmas in America. Where is the One God? At the cosmetic counters of Dillard's and Burdine's. If Jesus saw what they've done to him, the next time he would kill *himself*. Jesus' truth, if he has one, is Islam, not Christianity.

Florida was crazy with media hullabaloo because the Jews in Boca and West Palm Beach had voted for that goniff Bush without intending to; and as Florida went, America went, and Bush was president. They said he had thieved the election, and maybe he had. What had happened since, in and out of the courts, looked to me like a coup d'etat. But if America had been Syria or Iraq, Bush would have come in with tanks and had Gore shot in the basement of the Pentagon. There was something to be said for the subtler American way. Still, I noticed that Bush had stupid eyes, and that made me feel safe.

Al-Shibh had not found an American to give him a visa
in Yemen. He had tried one more time in Germany. He had
been denied again. We got an email from Jenny: "Our friend
Essabar will have to take my place. I am desolated. They will
not let me die!"

I was not pleased about Zacaria Essabar. He was a Moroccan
whom al-Shibh had introduced me to. He was haughty, and
arrogant, and I did not think it would be good to involve him
in our plan. In the end, it didn't matter because, two weeks
later, Jenny had emailed again. There had been a snag with
Essabar, too – *he* had been denied a visa. "What is the problem
with *him*?" Atta stormed. "He isn't Yemeni!"

It could be coincidence – or maybe not – that we were
hitting these roadblocks not so long after the attack on the
Cole; and, as I had learned from ABC News, America seemed
to know more about Sheikh Usama than it ought to have.
Atta never mentioned it, but I believed it possible that – in the
phrase of the TV cops I had grown up watching – we had been
"made." If we were caught, I realized, I would have lived a
wasted life, because it would be – practically – ended without
my having done *anything*. And that possibility frightened me
more than the fiery death I faced.

Jenny wrote that they had chosen another replacement
for her – Zacarias Moussaoui, another Moroccan mujihad.
Atta looked up from the email. "I know him. He was at the
Khalden camp when I was first in Afghanistan. A bald man

with a moustache and beard like you used to have, Marwan. He is not right for this mission. He is too emotional."

But the choice was not up to Atta, and so, over numerous emails and calls, Atta learned what he could from al-Shibh about our proposed fourth hand.

Moussaoui had been born in France of a bad marriage his mother had made when she was fourteen years old. Ten years later, the marriage had come to an end; Mrs. Moussaoui had crisscrossed France until she settled in Narbonne and began to make a good home for herself and her four children.

Moussaoui was a likeable boy, slow but full of good will, like the music of Bob Marley which he was addicted to. Unlike most boys of his age, he helped his mother make the beds, vacuumed and did the dishes – until they had a visitor, a cousin from Morocco, who told him these things were women's work, that he should behave like a man. He did not need much convincing. Soon he and his brother moved out.

He enrolled at a college in Montpelier, not far from Narbonne; then, on the spur of the moment, he removed himself to London. He had no money and knew no one there; for a time he lived in a homeless shelter. And yet somehow he managed to earn a master's degree in business. And begin a return to Islam, much as Atta had.

He grew a beard, changed his dress, went to London's radical mosques where the preachers were looking for candidates for Sheikh Usama. That led him to the Khalden camp, where Atta had run across him. There the Sheikh's recruits received basic training in weapons and hand-to-hand combat. He was a big, excitable man, and fit for that sort of thing.

Someone among the higher-ups must have seen something in him, because soon after al-Shibh began having trouble getting a visa, Moussaoui had gone to Kuala Lumpur, set up an email account and emailed the flight school in Norman, saying he would be in America within two weeks. Al-Shibh must have begged for more time to get himself a visa, because Moussaoui went back to England, not America. But after his fourth attempt failed, al-Shibh flew to London. Soon after he met with Moussaoui there, the Moroccan decamped for Afghanistan. We didn't know when to expect him. Al-Shibh said he would keep us informed.

We received our ratings and licenses in a charming little ceremony, and invited all our classmates to visit our palace in Riyadh. Preparing for what would follow, Atta, over the internet, bought flight deck videos for three Boeing planes and the Airbus. Our instructor had said these were medium to long range planes. They would be the ones to carry the load of fuel we needed. Uncertain whether, when the time came, we would know enough about navigation systems to point the planes where we wanted them to go, we made the drive to Fort Lauderdale and bought hand-held global positioners. Atta wanted to fly to Miami to try one out. And I thought: God, yes! Miami Vice!

For one last flight in Venice, we rented a plane from the flight school and headed east across the Everglades toward Miami International Airport. The GPS worked perfectly. It took signals from five satellites, fixed our position, and when Atta inputted Miami International's coordinates, it guided us toward our target on a virtual compass face. It was hardly any time at all until Miami slid into view. Pastel towers clustered along the shore of Biscayne Bay; huge cruise ships lay at the docks, and the bright wakes of Cigarettes sketched white lines out of the harbor toward the Bahamas and the Keys.

As we closed on downtown Miami, a sort of meditative look took over Atta's face. He held the stick steady a moment more, then banked the plane to the right.

"What are you doing, Atta?"

"I am going to fly at one of those buildings. See how it feels."

"Don't do it, cousin," I warned, feeling a bit of panic. "If anyone sees us – and somebody will – there will be a lot of questions when we get down."

Atta mulled it over. "Okay. You are right. I won't." He could be taken at his word, so I relaxed and looked down at the mansions on Star and Fisher Islands.

We set down to refuel the plane on Miami International's Runway 9L. Halfway down the taxiway, the engine stalled. After ten minutes of pushing buttons and plying the choke,

Atta pulled his cell phone out and called our former instructor, who told us to go see someone at the airport's general aviation contractor. We climbed out of the airplane and walked to their offices.

There was no one there who was useful, except for a secretary who, since she couldn't help with the plane, helped us rent a car. I begged Atta to detour through South Beach so I could see the rollerblading queens and the models in buttfloss thongs. Well – I didn't say what I wanted to see; I just said I would like to go. But Atta said we had better head back to the flight school right away.

The instructor tore out of his office as soon as we pulled up. "What the fuck are you doing? Where's my plane?"

Was Atta going to take this guff? "In Miami, on the taxiway. You gave us a lousy plane!"

"Oh yeah?" The instructor moved in close to Atta's nose. "They called me from Miami. There was nothing wrong with that airplane. You flooded it! And you didn't call the tower and let them know you were stuck on the taxiway!"

"Who knew to call the tower? There is no tower here, and I do not remember you mentioning anything about that when I called you while we were sitting there!"

"Because I assume if you are in my class you are not a complete moron! They had to route jets around that plane until they towed it off. And now I've got to send someone to Miami to fly it back."

"Good. He can take back our rental car. Which you owe us for."

"You can fucking forget it! And don't come here anymore!"

All right, we had done some stupid things – but we could fly! Now we needed to know how to pilot the big Boeing jets. To do that right would have taken years, a thousand hours of flying time, which we did not have. But all we really needed to learn, if everything went well, was to turn the planes, aim them, and descend to the height of the targets. Since we would have to be fools to assume that everything would go well, we also needed some practice in takeoffs, landings and bad weather flight.

For $1,500 we got all that on a 727 simulator at Opa-Locka Airport, outside of Miami. It was mounted on hydraulic legs, and it gave us not only the sights and sounds but also the sensations of each maneuver we ran through. We only had three hours each of time on the machine, but the basics of flying Boeings – turning, climbing, descending – do not, in principle, differ much from the planes we already knew.

We had to understand the Boeing's landing gear, their takeoff and cruising speeds, use of the autopilot and the yaw damper, how to set the navigation radios and the transponder .. a hundred little details. But it is amazing how much one can learn from a laptop-loaded Microsoft Flight Simulator. On that, while lying in our beds in the middle of the night, we could fly Boeings out of and into hundreds of actual airports, presupposing it was daytime or night, good weather or bad, and practice on all the factors we might come across. What we did not completely understand from either simulator we could study at our leisure in the aircraft handbooks we had, or the flight deck videos which showed the job done right.

I did get to see South Beach. It was less than I expected.

# 12

**Kandahar: November, 1999**

Marwan sat a while, just drifting. And then Atta walked in. "Well, well, Marwan," he grinned. "They let you live!"

Marwan was not surprised to see Atta. He had expected to. On the other hand, he no longer had a sense of time – so he had no way to judge how long he had waited for Atta, and that was what surprised him. "When did you get here?"

"I have been here for several days. Al-Shibh has just arrived. So now we can get to business."

What business was he talking about? Marwan had forgotten. Then he remembered. "Chechnya?"

Atta was pacing, back and forth, along the length of the mujihad inquisitor's table. Marwan thought he saw uncertainty in him. But then again, Marwan did not really know what he saw.

"No. We are not going to Chechnya." Atta stopped pacing and dropped into a chair across from Marwan. "I need to talk to you."

"Now?" Marwan whined. "Give me a break. I have not slept in five days!"

"I am sorry, Marwan. I want to discuss it now."

Marwan nodded, droopy-eyed. Atta would push on anyway.

"You know I am a builder, Marwan, not a destroyer. I would do anything to build a future for Islam …"

Marwan chuckled – or thought he did. "I was waiting for someone to mention that."

If Marwan had chuckled, it had not been infectious. "So was I, at first," Atta said. "Now I have come to understand that we will not have the chance to build anything until some things are gotten rid of. And I have found myself willing to destroy what must be destroyed."

"I see."

"But before we can take back what belongs to Islam, we must drive America out of the Muslim lands."

"Oh. That's simple," Marwan sighed. "How do you do that?"

"*We* do it, Marwan. *We* do it. It has been done already, in little ways. In Lebanon, one truck bomb and all the Marines went home. In Somalia, one helicopter downed and Clinton turned tail. But to do it all in one fell swoop, we must punish America. We must make the American people make their leaders do what we want. We must strike inside America. We have to hit them *hard!*" Atta was up and pacing again, emphasizing important words with quick jerks of his shoulders.

Marwan laughed. "What are you … what are *we* going to do? Blow up Washington?"

Atta was, almost imperceptively, quickening his pace. "You don't think we can do it? Have you heard of Ramzi Yousef? The man who set the explosion in New York, in the World Trade Center, seven years ago? He is in prison in America."

Yousef had been in all the news. But what had he accomplished?

"His uncle is with Sheikh Usama, right at the top. I met with the uncle when I came to Afghanistan before. He told me Yousef had other plans besides what he had done. He was going to blow up twelve American jets over the ocean, all at the same time. He had developed a microexplosive, tried it on a Philippine plane. Put it in a fellow's bag. The fellow did not know. It worked – it blew a big hole in the plane. The plane did not go down, but only because the pilot was a very capable man." The path of Atta's ellipses was tightening in.

"Another thing Yousef planned to do was to crash a plane into the headquarters of the American C.I.A. But then he had an accident. He was making bombs in Manila, and something caught fire. The police came. He got away, but they found explosive residue. The Americans caught him later. So none of it has been done."

Too bad, Marwan thought. How unhappy Yousef must be! Marwan thought he was being cynical. But he wasn't sure.

"It is the uncle's idea to put all these plans together into one. To hijack planes in America and crash them into buildings. At first, we thought into nuclear plants. But the uncle said we should not do that yet, so other targets were chosen. The World Trade Center, of course, to finish Yousef's work. And the White House. And the Capitol. And the Pentagon. All at once, in one blow, we destroy their leaders, we smash their financial power. For a time, they will be helpless. After that, they will understand that even worse things will happen to them if they do not leave Islam alone."

My friends are going to be terrorists, Marwan realized. Well … the things they have said, and the way they have behaved … I should have known.

"We will do to the Americans what they have tried to do to us. There is only one difference. They own an air force, and we will have to steal one. But we have the advantage there. Their air force costs them billions; ours costs us next to nothing. All we need is the will and the intelligence."

Even in his near-delirious state, Marwan understood the symmetry Atta saw in the plan. But the Americans would strike back. A lot of Muslims could die. He thought he was only thinking these things, but apparently he had said them.

"Strike back?" Atta chortled. "They will light candles! They will tie ribbons around trees! They will cry over people they could not have cared less about the day before, it's like crying at the movies, it keeps them entertained. But they will not risk more American lives. They will not fight."

"I would not bet on that," Marwan said. "If you ask *me*."

Exasperated, Atta plopped back into the chair. "Suppose you are right. What is the worst that they might do? What Clinton did after the embassies? We are an unseen enemy. They will not know where to hit! And if they kill a few of us, there will always be more! And suppose they send troops after us? We finished off the Russians; we will do the same to them. In the end, they will bring all their people home, and their puppets will drop like dominos!"

But the World Trade Center – Marwan said … All those innocent civilians …

The Yahoodis in those buildings, they are not innocent, Atta said. They control the money; they make America do what they want. No American is innocent, anyway. Their country is despoiling the world; their guilt is the same whether they play a part in it or do nothing to stop it. "And who do you think this idea came from? When the Americans dropped atom bombs on Hiroshima and Nagasaki, did they worry about civilians? Or did they target them, to make the people force the leaders to beg for peace!"

Atta reached out and grabbed Marwan's neck. He gave it a cousinly squeeze. "Listen, Marwan, it is perfect. We have figured out how to bring the towers down. We have videos of the buildings, and we know how they are built, because the engineer who built them testified at the trial of the Brothers who tried to blow them up before." It was architecture Atta was talking now, and he was exhilarated.

"Most skyscrapers are built on grids of steel columns, both interior and exterior, spaced every twenty or thirty feet – so if one of them fails, the others will take up the slack. But it costs a lot to do that, and it uses up floor space that otherwise could be rented. So the World Trade towers were not built like that. It is the outside columns – the facing – that carry a lot of their weight. Very few interior columns were used. I will not tell you all the details – they don't matter to you. But the steel in these columns, at the top of the buildings, is only a quarter inch thick. And instead of using heavy beams to support the floors, they used bar joist trusses, networks of thin steel bars. And they will melt at high heat, because the fireproofing they used is mineral wool, and they sprayed it on only half as thick as it should have been.

"Hit the towers high with planes, the planes will cut through the steel and spill their fuel, which will be on fire, down through the lower floors. The floor trusses will warp and snap, the exterior columns will buckle, and the floors will drop like a house of cards, one onto the other. Sheikh Usama thinks the planes can crash into three or maybe four floors. The floors above where they hit will collapse. And I think, with all that burning fuel, the whole building may come down.

"The stairwells are in the building's core, one next to the other; the fuel will spill down the stairways at two thousand degrees. The sprinkler pipes and water hoses are all fed from one place; when they hit the building, the planes will knock them out. And they did not use heavy masonry to protect the stairways from fire; they used gypsum, wallboards, it's good for fire but only if it stays intact, and the impact will knock at least some of the gypsum loose. No one will get out alive."

Oh, my, Atta, Marwan thought: You do hate America.

"The builders say the towers can withstand a 707. We will use larger planes, maybe 767's. Here is the business, Marwan. I am going to fly one of those planes. And I want you to fly the other one."

What a peculiar idea, Marwan thought. "I couldn't fly a kite into the World Trade Center …."

"You think I can? We will learn!"

Then Marwan remembered: Atta didn't make jokes.

"That is why I sent you here. Al-Shibh and I and the Fat Man, we chose you months ago."

Marwan plucked at his hair with his fingers, to pull the cotton out of his head. He couldn't quite get all of it; he was able to ask a question, but it wasn't the right one. "You have people to fly the other planes?"

"Al-Shibh and another man you haven't met. We are still looking for one more."

And then Marwan grasped what Atta was asking him to do. And he was able to ask the right question, but he really didn't need to, because he was clear and sober enough to answer it himself.

"How do we get out of these planes?"

"Please, Marwan," Atta answered him. "You know we do not."

"Did you say we were going to die, cousin?"

"There is no way out."

Marwan jumped up and beat on Atta with both fists. "Get out of here! *Fiq w'le*! Go fuck yourself! Leave me alone!"

"Marwan," Atta said evenly, fending off blows with his forearms, "the most important thing in life is how you die. To die for something outside yourself is the great thing. It is an honor. I want you to make the most of your life …"

Marwan kept hitting him. "A very short life!"

"No, not a short life!" Atta yelled. "If you do it, you will go to Paradise!"

"No." Marwan had heard enough. He put his fists away. "Go to hell. I like life. I'll think about Paradise later."

"Promise me you will consider it."

"Go away!"

# 13

## Spain: January, 2001

*En el nombre de Alá, el Compasivo, el Misericordioso*

I flew Delta to J.F.K., British Airways to London and on to Casablanca, then a little puddle jumper across the Straits of Gibraltar. Atta flew from Miami. Al-Shibh flew from Hamburg. Our bags were packed, for camouflage, with cologne and cigarettes.

We met in an apartment in a building with a doorman in a high-toned suburb on the south of Madrid. The apartment was done to Italian taste, which is mine as well – I used to study *Wallpaper*, the style magazine, planning the bachelor pad I would never get to create. Minotti sofas (cream leather), armchairs by Poltrona Frau, a plasma TV in a wall unit by B & B Italia. An oil like a low-rent El Greco glowed under halogen light – or maybe it was the real thing, I couldn't tell. The effect overall was of moderate wealth and a close-knit loving family,

109

the latter implied by the photographs propped up on console tables and the carpet of toys on which I nearly broke my neck while admiring the furnishings.

The used car salesman – it was his place – shot his cuffs at the entry way, showing good-sized slabs of lapis. The used car salesman did not sell cars – that was his cover story – but he had the sort of oily charm you expect from people who do. You just knew he would backslap a Christian, tell filthy jokes and guffaw at them, drink Spaniards under the table – and then return to this secret bastion of refinement and exhibit the behavior that really mattered to him.

His name was Abu Dahdah. His wife, a black-haired Spanish girl who had converted to Islam, un-Islamically greeted us at the door. Their four immaculate children were paraded for howdydo's and then, on their own hook, swiftly disappeared. Abu Dahdah assigned the three of us places on his Minottis. It was only then that I noticed three other men, in shiny beige suits and aviator shades, who were practicing a sort of movie-star lean against various walls and furniture.

Abu Dahdah folded his arms on his chest. "We are here to finance your mission. We need to know what you need."

Atta was going to answer him, but it was al-Shibh who did. "We need twenty more men. We need enough money to get them to America, then for food and places to live until the Day. We need money for the pilots, to do the same. Money to keep the pilots' flying skills up. Money for airline tickets, to get them all on the planes. Money to move them around in the States, wherever they are needed to be."

"Which comes to a total of what?" Abu Dahdah asked.

"Sheikh Usama thinks about a half a million dollars."

Abu Dahdah gathered the shiny suits. They talked feasibility. The only part of the suits that was moving was their mouths. I caught the Syrian dialect. They were all Aleppo men.

"Why do we need twenty more men?" This was Atta, who glared at al-Shibh.

"The Sheikh thinks we will need five men to take control of each plane."

The suits broke off their discussion. Abu Dahdah spoke. "You know there are other operations in motion besides yours."

"What kind of operations?" Atta said nastily. He was very angry, I believe, that there were things he had not yet been told, therefore things, perhaps, he might never be told, as if he were an assassin and not a holy man.

Abu Dahdah shrugged him off. "That is not for you to know."

"How many operations?" Atta kept on.

The salesman's back was up now, but al-Shibh stepped in. "Sheikh Usama believes that for the attack to have an impact, there must be multiple strikes."

Atta and I stared slack-jawed at our erstwhile roommate. What else did he know that we did not? And how did he know what Sheikh Usama thought and believed? And, come to think of it, exactly who *was* al-Shibh? And weren't all these airplanes "multiple" enough?

"How many strikes?" Atta asked al-Shibh.

"At least ten, close in time. And – uh – there are more pilots involved in your operation."

"I am aware of Moussaoui …" Atta began.

"Besides Moussaoui. They are on the west coast, in California."

Now Atta was livid. "Were you planning to tell me about them?"

"Yes," said al-Shibh. "Of course."

"When were you planning to tell me?"

"That is why you are in Spain."

The magnificent odor of saffron and fish came pouring out of the kitchen. Mrs. Dahdah brought out the paella in a huge, steaming bowl. The details were put aside for a glutton's hour and a half. It was while the chewing was in play that the salesman, who had sat me next to himself, leaned over and whispered to me. "Al-Shibh is very, very close to Sheikh Usama. I could see you did not know that. It is better that you do."

"I thought there was something about him," I said.

"Oh, you have no idea."

# 14

**Kandahar: November, 1999**

A mujihad brought Marwan back to his room. He had shut the door, but not locked it. If Marwan could get out of the house, he could hitch a ride with a smuggler, get back to Peshawar. Get rid of those beschädigt Afghani clothes. Find a way to get to Cairo. In case they might come after him, his mother would know someone who would shelter him.

He took off his shoes and tiptoed toward the door. He grabbed the doorknob – and it turned without his turning it. He let it go and jumped back, and in walked a short, rather chubby man in a white turban and robe. Light glinted on his glasses from a window in back of Marwan. "Forgive me for intruding. They call me The Doctor," he said. "I had thought you might be resting. Is there somewhere you wanted to go?"

Oh … no, Marwan told him. Just fidgety, is all.

"I have heard from your cousin," The Doctor said, "about

your quandary."

"I don't have a quandary. Atta has."

The Doctor's belly swelled as he sucked in air, then sighed it out. "The quandary is mine, I'm afraid. I need you. Do you mind if I rest these old bones? I am very tired."

"Sure. Of course. My pleasure," Marwan said. The Doctor's knees protested as he folded onto the bed.

"I believe this mission calls for even-minded men. Most of the men who come to us are inclined to be ... excitable." The Doctor chuckled a moment. "Passion is good – don't misunderstand – but it tends to ... cloud the judgment. This job will require precision, and that is not to be expected from a man who is on the brink of a death he is longing for. I believe your cousin can manage it – he is motivated properly. He does not do this for himself, but for all of us, for Islam. It is not an impulse; he has thought it through. He is absolutely determined." He tapped a finger at a temple. "He has the analytical mind, he is dispassionate. In fact, I suspect he is a total stranger to infatuation. Ha. I would not want to marry him, but I would trust him with my life."

Atta had said The Doctor was a man without remorse. But he spoke very sympathetically, and he looked sort of cute and cuddly. It might have been bedside manner. But he had perfected it.

"Al-Shibh ... well ..." He pursed his lips. "You know, I would put myself on this mission if I were not needed here. I will gladly undergo martyrdom when it is necessary. But I do not court it. Al-Shibh does. I don't know why he wants it so badly. It bothers me … But he drives himself ferociously, and he will drive all of you. I just don't know what will happen if you do not succeed, and he lives …"

He seemed to be turning that over. Then he said: "I believe you are … matter of fact." He dropped a surprisingly delicate hand on Marwan's knee. "You study reality. So I think you will bring us a measure of common sense – and God knows we will need it before this thing is done. And I also think …" He took his hand away. " … that once you come to grips with it, you will manage it easily."

Oh yes. It will just be another final exam. You will be brilliant, son.

"I want you to understand that what we are asking you to do will remake the universe. It will bring down America, and restore the world to Islam. You will all be the martyrs of martyrs, the catalysts of Fate. No Muslim has done more for the faith than you will do. I would place you with the Prophets, if it were not blasphemy. And all of Islam will know it. You will be eternal in their eyes."

"Yes," Marwan said. "But, you see …"

"I could say you would be eternal in fact, but I am not sure you would believe me."

"I hope there is a Paradise. But you understand: I'm like you. I don't want to go there yet."

"So you are afraid to die."

Well, yes, Marwan thought – that is *normal*. In fact, I should be allowed, like every other boy, to believe for as long as possible that I will *never* die.

"That is the price of your lack of faith. If you want to overcome that fear, you will have to work at it."

Marwan promised himself he would not let The Doctor talk him around. But The Doctor was so avuncular, and he was so very tired.

"It isn't fair to ask me this. I'm too young."

The Doctor nodded. "Yes, you are very young. But tell me, what else could you do with your life that would accomplish as much?"

"Maybe nothing," Marwan answered, "but there are other reasons to live."

"Then let me put it another way." The Doctor turned so that Marwan could see his eyes. He wasn't so cuddly now. "What else do you have to look forward to? If they find out that you knew Atta … and that you have been to Afghanistan … you will be lucky if they do not track you down and murder you." His eyes went frosty; he shook his head. "And we will not protect you, if you turn us down.

"You will have no career in Europe, you can forget about that. After this, no Muslim will. You will have to find work in the Muslim world. But what could you do? Masonry, that is possible. Or putting up telephone poles. Or you could be a head waiter. That sounds rewarding to me. And everyone around you will have contempt for you, because they will know you could have helped them, and you refused.

"Then," he said, "on the other hand, this I promise you. If you do it, we will care for your mother for the rest of her days."

He reached out and lifted Marwan's hands. "So – you hold the future of Islam. I beg you, Marwan, do not tell me you will let it fall …."

# 15

**Dubai: January, 2001**

---

The funds the Syrians arranged came mostly from Saudi Arabia, and were to be funneled to us through the Emirates – not the Sharjah hawala, though, but a real bank in Dubai. So Atta and I flew from Spain to Dubai to talk to the money man. While standing in the entry line at Dubai immigration, I caught a glimpse of Jarrah in another line. I had not known Jarrah would be there. I didn't know why he was.

I found out after I checked in that Jarrah was staying, under his real name, at the same hotel as we were, the Intercontinental Dubai on BinYas Street. In the lobby, away from Atta, I rang up Jarrah's room. I invited him to dinner. He said he would come. We met in the Boulvar restaurant, one of the hotel's eight, and after we were seated we leaned over the table top to avoid being eavesdropped on.

"They almost arrested Atta at the airport," I said. "He was

on some sort of terrorist list."

"I saw him arguing with Customs," Jarrah replied.

"They checked with the U.S. Embassy to see if there were charges. Can you imagine: our Arab brothers are helping the F.B.I.!"

"Yes, I can imagine. That's why we are doing what we are. Were there any charges?"

"No."

Jarrah looked relieved.

"But now U.S. immigration will be watching out for him."

Jarrah snorted. "Don't be ridiculous. They have no idea where anyone is – and I don't think they care."

"Okay," I said. "I hope you're right. So, Ziad – why are you here?"

Jarrah's eyes narrowed; he studied my face. Then his head went down to his folded hands. "I've been to see my father. He's sick. It's his heart. They're going to operate on him next month."

"Sorry," I said.

"Thanks, my friend."

"You saw him in Dubai?"

"No, in Lebanon, of course."

"And so you are in Dubai because ….?

Jarrah caught my eyes again. "I came here to … " His shoulders went up. "Ah, who knows?"

"Ziad, are you spying on Atta and me? Don't they trust us?"

"Oh my God, Marwan," he laughed, slapping his palms on the table. "You are such a little boy. It's not that you are not trusted. It's just that you have to be watched. Why, aren't you and Atta watching me?"

"No one told me to."

"Well, Atta is."

"He knew you were going to be here?"

"Yes, of course." He leaned closer. "But he doesn't know everything."

"What do you mean?" I asked him.

Jarrah attempted to look contrite, but could not quite manage it. "I brought my girlfriend to Florida."

"You did *what*?"

"She was angry she hadn't seen me," he grinned. "She's always mad at me. Why are women so difficult? I had to let her come. I rented a plane," he giggled. "We flew to the Florida Keys. I got a Conch Republic passport."

"Conch Republic?"

"The Conch Republic. That's what they call Key West."

"What is a conch?"

"Some sort of snail. I ate it. It was good. It was also good to spend a few nights between my girlfriend's legs."

"What are you doing, Ziad?" I sighed. "Does it make any sense?"

"Oh God," Jarrah moaned, his normal glee suddenly vanished. "I took her as a passenger in that Boeing simulator in Miami, you know, practicing for .. you know what for. She thinks it's for my career. And I'm thinking to myself, what the hell are you doing, man? It's like I know I'm going to fly the plane, yet I don't seem to realize what I'm going to do with it … But Marwan, can you imagine yourself not … being around? I mean, who can do that? I *know*, but I can't comprehend it. I mean – I want my girlfriend, not seventy-two virgins. I never liked virgins anyway." He shook his head. "Ah. Ignore me. I am full of shit today."

But Jarrah could not stop himself. "I mean, do you know how weird it is … When we started seeing each other, we had to hide it from her parents, because … they were so orthodox. And then I get serious about Islam …"

"*Are* you serious, Ziad?" I asked. "I mean, do you really believe?"

"Yes. Of course. But she wouldn't … wasn't … interested. I asked her to cover herself up. She looked at me like I was nuts. I didn't push her, so … I mean, we … made plans. Tried not to talk about Islam. But we fight all the time."

"Have you told her you are going to marry her?"

"My family already gave us a car for a wedding present. It's waiting for me in Lebanon."

"What are you …"

"We talk about kids."

"Ziad … for God's sake … "

"I don't know, Marwan. I love her. Hey. The Conch

Republic passport? I got it in Atta's name." He started to laugh. It was catching. But I was not sure about Jarrah. I thought I recognized in him something I had seen in myself.

There was something else I had to know. "You met al-Shibh in Yemen last summer. Was it because of the Cole?"

"That destroyer that got blown up? Me? No! Are you crazy? What do I know about that?"

# 16

**Kandahar: December, 1999**

---

The commander, Abu Hafs al-Khebir, was dressed in a camo suit. He was Egyptian, like The Doctor. His daughter, they said, was married to Sheikh Usama's son.

"You will get no hands-on training from us," he said, as a beginning. "What we can teach you, you do not need to know. And we do not want other brothers to be aware of you. That is why you are in this place, and not one of our larger camps. Of course, you will need specialized training. We will let the Americans do it. They are so cooperative."

A young man whom Marwan did not know sat listening along with the other three. His long face was bright like a gleeful boy's, though bearded and heavily eye-browed. He was tall and athletically built; even when he was sitting still, he seemed to be in motion.

"For the time you are here," the commander went on,

"you will focus on what we require of our members. If you have any deficiencies, you will rectify them.

"You must be a Muslim." Here the commander's eyes pinned Marwan. "No unbeliever can protect Islam, and defend its goals and secrets. You will be committed to our ideology. This eliminates the need for thinking about anything but how to accomplish your mission. You will be reconciled with martyrdom. You will behave like soldiers, because that is what you are. You will follow orders without question. You will reveal nothing of anything to anyone. You will remain free of illness. You will be patient in your work, in case of complications. You will be tranquil and unflappable. You will calmly contemplate and endure arrest, imprisonment, or the killing of any or all of your comrades, or of yourself. You will use your intelligence. You will be cautious and prudent. You will be truthful to the brothers, and false to all else.

"You will memorize the documents which are given to you. We will test you on them. You will study alone. You will not debate amongst yourselves. *Am I clear?*"

"Aiwa! Ehna fahimnah!" Yes! We understand!

"Allah-hu akhbar! Death to the Jews!"

Atta, al-Shibh, Ziad Jarrah and Marwan shouted the phrases back.

Marwan spent weeks on the parts of the manual they wanted him to read. They were mostly on religious themes

– suras and hadiths and fatwas that assured them that it was permitted and right to do what they planned to do. And he lifted and opened the Qur'an as often as he had time. Those words that had lost their meaning for him now were directing his fate, so he was working hard to remember how simple and sure his life had been when he had loved Allah. He found peace in some of the passages, things that settled him down, brought him through those midnights when he was sure he was going insane. Maybe, he began to think, it was when life was complicated that you needed to love Allah – and when you had to do things you were not sure were good, it was soothing … it was helpful to know that Allah approved of those things. "*Little do you remember how many a city We have destroyed! And their cry, when Our terror came to them, was: Surely we were unjust.*"

He only saw his brothers at the five daily salats. No speaking was permitted except for the words of the prayers. But one night, as they stood shoulder to shoulder on al-Shibh's Afghani baluch, Ziad Jarrah nudged him. "Are you all right?" he whispered.

Why does he ask, Marwan wondered? Do I look unsure? I mean, he doesn't know me. What does he see? "Yes, I'm good," he whispered back. "What about you?"

"Oh, yes, I love it! This is serious stuff! It's great!"

So Marwan envied Jarrah, and wanted to be like that.

In the end, the four of them were brought together once

ore. They sat in the little classroom, not knowing what to expect. A few minutes later The Doctor strode in, papers in his hands.

"Brothers," he instantly began – giving Marwan the slightest nod. "It is the essence of Islam that all of us are one community. '*And hold fast all together by the rope of Allah and be not divided among yourselves.*'"

The head of the Hamburg taxiruf driver flashed into Marwan's mind. It said: "This man is a fucking ass hole, there is no unity." Marwan waggled his head furiously to chase the driver out. But the head of the Shi'ite stayed there. "You who fuck your mothers!" Marwan conjured up a burlap bag, and showed it to the Shi'ite, who went off to bother someone else and left Marwan alone.

" … That community is the khilafa, the caliphate. And there can be no community without a leadership, an imam to execute the rules, proclaim what conduct is right, equip the armies, punish those who rebel, judge in matters of dispute, and distribute the wealth we gain through jihad fairly among all."

The Doctor paced the edge of the room, always turned toward the team.

"From the day of the death of the Prophet – peace be unto him – all Islam was unified under the rule of a khalifa, the heir to Allah's Messenger. There was always a khalifa, one following the other, until the year 1924 in the Julian calendar. Then this authority was destroyed by the British and the traitor Mustafa

Kemal, and divided among ruling regimes of so-called "nation states," which were made by the unbelievers, were imposed upon us by force, betrayal, oppression and deception, and have worked for the unbelievers, executing their orders. We are in the time of fitna, of mischief and evil works.

"But we – and I include you most particularly – will turn the tables over the heads of these depraved and treacherous rulers. We will establish the khilafa state over all of Islam. A khalifa will once again rule over all, by that which Allah has revealed. He will declare jihad to uproot the Jews, and remove all infidel influence from every hand span of the Muslim's land. And he will carry Islam to the world as a message of guidance and light.

"Obedience to the khalifa comes next after obedience to Allah and to his Messenger. '*And whoever gives a baya'a, a pledge of allegiance, to an imam, giving him the clasp of his hand and the fruit of his heart, shall obey him as long as he can.*' Because there is no authority without hearing and obeying.

"But now there is no caliph. So, until there is, every Muslim must swear allegiance to an emir. Because, as we are told in the hadith of Abdullah ibn Umar, the Prophet – peace be upon him – has said that he who dies without a baya'a in his neck will die in jahiliyya, in a state of sin.

"Your emir is Sheikh Usama. You will swear baya't to him. '*And if another comes to dispute with him, you must strike the neck of that man.*'

"You know what trust we place in you. But we must go beyond trust, to absolute certainty that you will do your utmost to fulfill your mission. If you do, Allah will ensure that you succeed. Two of you signed this before. This is for the others."

The Doctor walked stiffly to Jarrah and Marwan, handing each a paper. It committed them to loyalty unto death to the person of Sheikh Usama. He pulled from his pocket a pen for each. "You will sign," he said. They did.

The Doctor took back the papers and turned toward the door. "Someone wants to speak with you," he said.

And then, bending his head low, since he was too tall for the doorway, entered the most beautiful man Marwan had ever seen, the seventeenth son, the fifty-fourth child of a multibillionaire. He towered over the rest of them, dressed all in white. His smile was beatific, his eyes downcast. A golden aura flowed from him; he looked like a halo-headed saint in an Italian renaissance painting. He put his hands together in the posture of prayer, and The Doctor found himself a place three steps behind.

"My brothers," said Sheikh Usama, "I welcome you to jihad." His smile grew larger. Marwan attended breathlessly.

"America does not want Islam to remain on the face of this planet. Under Jewish Zionist blackmail, America has incited massacres of Muslims all over the world. They compromise our honor and our dignity, and dare we utter a single word of protest against this injustice, we are called terrorists. They reduce Muslims to peons, who come to the cities and lose themselves, and have no clan and no dignity, and do not know who they are. And no one will help them except ourselves – we feed them and clothe them, take care of them when they are sick, and when they are old. We will tell them who they are. They are Muslims. And if they return to Islam, they will find themselves.

"But it is not just to Muslims that we speak. We extend an invitation to all the nations to embrace our religion, which calls for justice, mercy and fraternity, not differentiating between black and white or between red and yellow, except as to how devotedly they cling to Allah.

"And this is what America fears – that, and our revenge. America can be kept at bay by blood alone. And so we have issued a fatwa that to kill them and their allies is a duty for every Muslim everywhere, in accordance with the words of Almighty Allah: '*Fight them until there is no more tumult or oppression, and there prevail justice and faith in Allah.*'

"Americans are the most filthy sort of human beings! For what they have done to the Muslim peoples, we will – because we have the right – kill four million Americans – two million of them children – and exile twice as many and cripple hundreds of thousands more. We shall destroy their union; we shall split them into separate states, as they have done to us. Furthermore, it is our right to use any sort of weapons, because of the weapons they have used on us.

"Our enemies protect their lives like a miser protects his money. They do not enter battles seeking martyrdom. What is important to them is to continue to live, even a mortifying life, being kicked or whipped on their backsides. But you – you do not need to protect your lives. Allah has promised you two great things: triumph and martyrdom. '*If you stand by Allah, He will stand by you.*'"

He smiled and held out both his hands. They jumped up, circled around him and kissed the hands each in his turn. He reached down and touched Marwan's face. The skin was hot under his hand.

Marwan was back in Hamburg for "New Year's Eve," the "Dawn of the Millennium." The TV showed celebrations "all over the world." They showed nothing in Cairo, or in Istanbul, or Beirut. The Christian calendar begins on the date of the birth of Christ. The Islamic calendar goes forward from the day of the hijra – July 16, 622, by Christian reckoning – when the Prophet went to Medina and Islam was born. Each new month begins with the rise of the crescent moon, so there are twelve months to the Islamic year, but only three hundred and fifty four days. To Marwan, January 1$^{st}$, 2000 was the twenty-fourth day of the ninth month of the year 1420.

So it was not his New Year's Eve. It was not his Millennium. But, insh'Allah, he thought, it would be – in a very different sense.

# 17

## Hollywood, Florida: March, 2001

A cop pulled Atta over outside of Fort Lauderdale. He was going a little too fast – something he never did – and cursed himself for drawing attention to himself. He had no U.S. drivers' license; none of us did. His license was Egyptian. The cop was going to take him in, since he could not prove Florida residence and Florida cops are sensitive about tourists who earn traffic tickets, go home and "forget" to pay them. But my sweet disposition calmed the officer – anyway, he had a quota to make and he did not want to waste time at the station house with Atta.

The next day we both got licenses. There was no trick to that. There are people driving in Florida who can't see over the wheel.

We flew practice hours in February out of Briscoe Field, an airport twenty miles northeast of downtown Atlanta, Georgia.

On the dark nights of our fourteen days in a Georgia motel, we studied the airline schedules Atta had collected. Because we needed big planes with big fuel loads, we had to find flights out of East Coast airports headed for California. Because we wanted the targets hit at just after nine in the morning, when most of the people who worked in them were at their desks, we had to work backward from that time, factoring in taxi time at departure and arrival based on the typical traffic at each airport at each time of year; factoring in weather delays based on the same sorts of data; providing for the on-time departure rates of all the major airlines, the time it would take to subdue the crew, and the time it would take to reverse the plane and get back to the target area. It was a complicated formula, concocted by Atta and me, based on data we picked up on the internet. It turned out there were not a lot of flights that fit our paradigm. But we only needed five. We found more than that.

In March, when Jarrah came back from Lebanon after his father's surgery, he rented a tiny white bungalow with cast iron trim near Federal Highway in the town of Hollywood, just below Fort Lauderdale on Florida's southeast coast. Atta and I moved to Hollywood, too, shortly after Jarrah – first to the Bimini Motel, a two story joint, forty dollars a night, one of a string of cheap motels along the intracoastal waterway. The manager spoke German, which made for *gemütlichkeit*. A certain class of Germans made a habit of Hollywood, like the

British who love the Spanish coast and wreck it every summer – *fußbalspeiler*, maniacs, *griese on altersrente*. We moved from there, when we had had enough, to a second-floor dump a mile and a half from the place that Jarrah had leased, on one of the streets named for American presidents that bracket Hollywood Boulevard, the city's east-west main drag.

We had chosen southeast Florida because it was more cosmopolitan than the Gulf Coast had been – more different kinds of people, more nationalities, more people in general. We would be less conspicuous. Suspicion was not normal in Florida anyway. People were friendly and open; they left their doors unlocked.

Hollywood was an awful place – hideous old retirement complexes crumbling of their own weight, their miniscule screened-in balconies crammed with the lower order of octogenarian Catholics and Jews; a failed downtown revival, raucous French-Canadians whose condos and bungalows clustered on the beach like a women's sewing circle. But what better place, we decided, to live anonymously, until the day when we wanted the world to know our names?

It was not that I did not question living in Hollywood. I had driven north to West Palm Beach and looked at Cityplace, a brand-new ersatz Siena. Apartments, shops, restaurants and assorted bright night venues were piled up around a piazza with a clocktower built by a toy store and a fountain that threw dancing water jets twenty feet high. But Atta would have none of it. "The heart dies of fun," he said.

There was really nothing to do then; we were waiting for our next move. I spent my Hollywood time prowling the streets. Even in season, no one walks in Hollywood except where the shops and restaurants are, strung westward off the beach. Wander a little farther west – towards the house we were living in – and there was nothing live on the pavement except palmetto bugs.

But even without the multitudes, and with mostly one story shacks, a faint air of Peshawar floated over the town. It was untended, beaten down, so far past its palmy days that, outside of a museum, those days were not credible.

As long as I had kept busy, I had not had to think about what all my activity was leading me to. I had planned my life one day at a time, doing what was assigned to me, then moving on to the next task, never shifting the focus further ahead than that. But Hollywood was boring … and thoughts I would rather not have had started creeping into my head. There were times I found myself quivering, and I could not seem to stop it. The doubts had to run their course, then dive under the ennui; because if they kept bothering me, I was not sure what I would do …

It was in one of these dark moments that Atta announced that we were going to fly to Las Vegas to meet the West Coast cell. Sheikh Usama, al-Shibh had emailed, had changed the plan. At first there were going to be ten planes, five on the East

Coast and five on the West, but something – al-Shibh had not said what – had gotten too complicated. Now it was down to five East Coast planes, and the crews were to be combined.

Right away I felt better. If it is true that the heart dies of fun, I thought, I am going to have an infarction when the end of May rolls around and we hit the Vegas strip.

# 18

**Hamburg: January, 2000**

---

The al-Quds majlis was on the second floor of a building in Hamburg Steindamm. It was above a Vietnamese restaurant and a gym, the smells of both of which wafted through the mosque from time to time. The building was one of those modern boxes of no character with which the West is everywhere filled and which have sprung up in the Arab world as well – the kind that enraged Atta because he despised them as an Islamist *and* as an architect. The walls and the carpet were turquoise in the men's prayer room, a mix of green – the color of Islam – and blue – the color of heaven. The women's room was off to one side. You could barely look into it.

Bahaji's grin nearly split his round face when he saw his bride-to-be – though of course there was not very much of her to be seen. Marwan had met her on one of his earlier visits to Atta's flat. She had worn a miniskirt. It had driven al-Shibh crazy, and Atta too. They would rather have walked into walls than lift their eyes and see her. Not Marwan. He liked those skirts. He assumed she had given them away, since she would never wear another.

But she had gotten Bahaji to agree in the nikah – the marriage contract – that he would not take another wife, though the Qur'an allowed him four, and that she could divorce him if she wanted to. So maybe, Marwan thought, she had stashed the miniskirts in her father's house, against the day when she might want to put them on again.

Imam al-Fazazi conducted the marriage ceremony. It was Fazazi Marwan had seen on Atta's VCR. The Prophet had provided words to be used, relating to marital rights, but Fazazi could not resist the chance to rail against the Jews, so he went a little far afield for the happy circumstances:

"They have butchered our children, widowed our women and defiled our holy places! Wherever you meet Jews, kill them! As Allah the Almighty said: '*Fight them; Allah will torture them at your hands.*' And kill the Americans, too, who midwifed this miserable Israel in the beating heart of the Arab world, to be the outpost of their culture and the vanguard of their army, the sword of the Crusaders, hanging over our necks! By the way, there is a marriage, and I want to say …"

The sermon rolled off Marwan's back, and Atta said nothing about it. But Bahaji and al-Shibh got into the spirit of the thing. Bahaji yelled and shook his arms, with fists at the end of them. "The Jews will burn, and we are going to dance on their graves!" Al-Shibh's non-alcoholic toast was a paean to jihad. Not til they had all expressed themselves could the wedding be performed; then the desert trill of the women signaled the union was complete until Bahaji or – in this case – his wife decided enough was enough.

For the fifty or sixty male guests, the bride's father had spread a walima feast which, after the nuptials, Marwan attacked, since he had been up before dawn for the salat-ul-Fajr, Atta as usual had no food and he was half starved to death. Two lambs had been slaughtered; lamb stew and shawarma, baked plums, almonds, sweet cakes and lemonade were piled on a long wooden table with a white linen tablecloth.

Marwan was loading up his second plate when Atta pulled him away. "I want you to meet somebody." He guided another man toward Marwan, a strange-looking fellow who wore his hair longer than most of them, pomaded back at the brow, so that he looked like Little Richard, except that he was bearded, and he had bad teeth. Like the rest of the men in Atta's group, he had made an attempt for the wedding to dress in the Western style, so as not to alert the other guests by his clothes to his tendencies. But he did not have the cash to do it well, and the suit didn't … didn't suit him. He was a student at TU Harburg, in electrical engineering, as Bahaji was and Marwan would be in a day or two.

"I have lived in Hamburg for five years," Bad Teeth said,

"so if you need any help getting around, I mean with where things are …"

"Thank you," said Marwan. "If I do …"

Before he could get out another word, another man approached them, dressed to kill – metaphorically – in the right kind of dark blue suit set off by an Hermes tie and gold and opal cuff links. He put an arm around Atta, gave Bad Teeth a wink and discreetly slipped a business card into Marwan's hand. "What I do is ship electronics to Syria and Jordan. Call me Abu Ilyas. Don't use the name on the card." Marwan judged the man was Syrian, from the patterns of his speech.

"Can I get a new TV from you?"

"Sorry. Only wholesale." But in a rumbling conspiratorial tone the man went on. "There may be other things I can do for you."

And then the Fat Man sidled up and clapped Marwan on the shoulder. The weight of his hand was so immense Marwan nearly buckled under it. No suit in the world would have fit that frame, so his dress was Western casual, except for the Arafat head scarf curled around his neck. He crushed the hand of Abu Ilyas, who winced and walked away. "Good wedding, hah?" he said. "You are ready to go, Marwan, yes? We cannot just sit and do nothing."

Marwan said: "Yes, I am ready."

"So, then, you will excuse me? They are running out of lamb."

Marwan went to introduce himself to the father of the bride, who was standing rather forlornly off to himself, ignored by Atta's coterie, not "one of us." "My daughter rides horses," he sighed. "She loves to dance. I do not know why she is marrying this man."

But by then, the sun had gone down. The song of the brothers' prayers rose up, and that was the end of the wedding.

# 19

## Las Vegas, Nevada: March, 2001

So cheesy – but, oh, magnificent! From the cab windows on the ride from McCarran Airport, half a billion twinkling lights; cars that made your saliva run out of control; millions of women in tiny clothes, available. All my adolescent dreams an arm's reach away.

Atta arrived before I did, and checked us into the Travelodge at the cheap north end of the Strip above Sahara Avenue, next door to a bungee-jumping park and The Guinness World Records Museum. When he came to the room door to let me in, his eyes were dull and lifeless, and his mouth was hanging open. He looked like a man with battle fatigue, and I knew why: the sins he had seen on the drive into town had sent him into shock.

He forcibly forbade me to hit the streets that night. The next morning we moved to another motel two blocks off the Strip, a three-story establishment that could have been anywhere: no pets, no kids, no fun. Atta never left the room; the West Coast men came to us.

When they did, I glanced at the mirrored wall in the room's foyer – Las Vegas elegance – and caught a portrait of all of us. I realized there was nothing about us – except for Atta's eyes – that would raise goosebumps on the arms of any American. We did not have the Semitic hooked nose or the beards of the religious. We were dressed like any Westerner – well, maybe a little bit better. Nawaf al-Hazmi, with his short curly hair, dark skin and full but well-trimmed moustache, might have been Italian, or Mexican. Khalid al-Midhar, square-jawed and well-built, could have starred in a soap. Little Hani Hanjour – of decent height for a Saudi, maybe five foot six, but mercilessly underweight, like a balding stalk of asparagus – could have been the weak-faced boy your peripheral vision sometimes caught standing at the edge of the crowd in a blues café.

As al-Shibh had explained in Spain, al-Midhar had been born a Yemeni, but was now a Saudi citizen. He had worked on the Red Sea as a fisherman. His wife was somehow related to al-Shibh. The other two were native-born Saudi Arabians.

Al-Midhar and al-Hazmi had already done other things. Al-Shibh had met them in Kuala Lumpur after we left Afghanistan – that meeting involved our mission, and others he would not discuss. For over a year, al-Midhar and al-Hazmi had been living in San Diego. They had taken flying lessons there, and behaved themselves appropriately for the neighborhood, buying tickets to Sea World, and taking limos to sex shows at one o'clock in the morning. Al-Hazmi was placing classified ads for a Mexican mail-order bride; al Midhar had left his wife behind, and was paying two or three girls a week to do the only things he enjoyed of what she had done for him.

Those two sprawled into the brown plaid sofa. Hanjour perched himself fragilely on the edge of a brown plaid chair. I lay stomach down on the brown plaid bedcover. There followed a sort of chicken dance as Atta, who would not sit at all, kept adjusting his posture in accord with his perception – which varied from moment to moment – of who in the room was in charge of things: him, or al-Midhar.

"We have rented a place in New Jersey," al-Midhar said. "We will be taking the Newark flights. You two will be taking Boston."

The comment uplifted Atta at first. It was he and I who had chosen those two departure points. But someone else had decided the city from which he would fly – and that did not sit well with him. "And who has made this pronouncement?" he wanted to know.

"It comes from the commander." And that was that.

Some of the other men we needed had already arrived. Al-Midhar had secreted them in a Connecticut motel, then moved them to New Jersey, where they were waiting now. The rest were expected to fly in within two weeks. Some were coming to Florida, direct from Kandahar. We would have to put them up. We had better get busy with that.

"And what about Moussaoui?" Atta asked.

"He is in Oklahoma, at that flight school," said al-Midhar. "We went out to see him. What an idiot. He managed to pass the pilot's exam, but they would not let him solo. They were afraid of what he would do to their plane. He is looking for another school, but I would not count on him."

That was really all there was – just passage of information. If the plan was for us to get comfortable with each other, it didn't work for Atta, not then or at any time. We had a moment of common ground saying our prayers together – that was the first occasion I had had to hear Hani Hanjour speak. But these West Coasters were Beduin – of the tribes that knew the Prophet. To them, Atta was a parvenu; they would not show him respect because he had come late by ten centuries to the Arabian point of view.

As the three West Coasters rose to leave, Atta announced he was hungry. Al-Midhar gave him a lazy gaze, meaning: So what?

"I will not leave this building, and this hotel has no food."

Al-Midhar raised his eyebrows, meaning: And so?

"I would like you to get us something."

Al-Hazmi laughed out loud.

"I'll go," I told Atta. Please please please.

"No," he scowled. Then: "Go ahead." Atta rarely let me go out alone – he had orders, I suspected, to keep a close eye on me – but how else was he going to eat?

I followed the three of them out of the room. Hanjour quickly disappeared. The other two hit the pavement, making for the Stratosphere, the only casino close to my prison of a motel and right next door to the St. Louis Manor where al-Midhar and al-Hazmi theoretically slept. I tagged along with them. On the way down Las Vegas Boulevard, tempting females wiggled past – although here, at the crummy end of the Strip, they might have been something else; you never knew if what you were looking at was a *stricherin* or a *stricher*. The other two's heads kept whipping around – left, then right, then left. "Holy shit," I heard al-Hazmi sigh. "Holy shit! Holy shit! Holy shit!"

The Stratosphere Casino is a massive white building in the tropical style, with two wings bent at thirty degrees off the center structure, and a 109-story free-standing tower streaked with blue and pink neon and topped with a rotating restaurant like the one that is in Seattle. The Strat-O-Fair Midway wandered around the base of the tower; and above this mélange of roller coasters and virtual bowling, near the top of the tower, was something called the Big Shot. Al-Midhar pointed up at it. "We do that," he said.

A thousand feet above the earth, on a metal mesh structure that rose above the rotating restaurant, we strapped ourselves into four-abreast seats that hung out into space. When the seats shot up to the tower's top like a space shuttle launch, my stomach went up into my throat and I lost lunch. As we dropped back to the starting point, al-Midhar and al-Hazmi brushed it off onto the people below, and shook their heads in disgust.

Then the damned thing shot up again, and I was not okay. Coming down for the second time, I lacked trust in fate, and in that I was justified, because it rocketed up again and this time when the rocketing stopped I flew into the seat restraint, clear out of my chair. But my friends, the Arab astronauts, were as happy as *schweine in kot*. "After this," al-Hazmi giggled, "flying a Boeing into a wall will not be anything."

"Except you will be dead at the end of it," I managed to get out.

"*Zib umak, ya khawal*. I will be fucking my brains out in Paradise."

"Let's eat," said al-Midhar. I could not conceive of it. They wanted to do it up royally in the rotating restaurant, but I refused to go near anything that was not standing still. The hotel had a Mexican place called the Crazy Armadillo. They had developed a taste for Mexican food living in San Diego, and once I had calmed my stomach down I found it appealed to me – until two bartenders went into their act, juggling three bottles of tequila while filling a shooter from each. The whirling disrupted what was left of my equilibrium. When I returned from the bathroom, half-naked girls were on the bar and al-Midhar and al-Hazmi were stuffing dollars into their thongs.

The sight of money in Arab hands attracted the attention of two blondes with appendaged watermelons and legs of serious length. There is a question of Islamic belief, as yet unresolved, as to whether when one is in Paradise one's erection is ever-present, or only on demand. Al-Midhar and al-Hazmi, I thought, whatever the rule was in Paradise, would have hardons that never abated and were constantly drawn upon.

There was another way in which these two were not like the rest of us. They were cold, like the men in Kandahar, the mujahidin who would not think twice about snapping somebody's neck. You knew they had already killed – and not in some small way. You knew they had snuffed out lives one-on-one, and carried out larger plans.

But the mujahidin in Kandahar killed to glorify Allah. Al-Midhar and al-Hazmi were in no way unsoiled Muslims, so I assumed that what drove them was another sort of passion: a sensual pleasure they derived either from hate, or from death. And I could imagine their ecstasy at being included in our mission – how orgasmic they thought the end would be, that they would give up their lives to feel it.

The blondes negotiated. Then al-Midhar waved at me. "Hey, Ras al Khaimah dog – do you want in on this?"

I strolled over casually – though the truth is I was in rapture over the mere thought of a fuck. And a third girl, dark-haired, with a merciless look in her eye, climbed off a barstool and wandered into the group. "Want some fun?" she asked me.

"Sure," I said. "How much?"

"If you have to ask me, honey," she smiled, "you prob'ly can't cover it."

"Oh yes? Do you take credit cards?"

"Absolutely," she said.

But then I remembered Atta. I had not got his food. The Saudis concluded arrangements and left the restaurant. I picked up a turkey sandwich at the Triple Crown Deli and took it back to Atta. It was nearly three a.m. Atta did not thank me – just gobbled the sandwich down.

# 20

## Munich: February, 2000

---

Marwan would not have chosen that month to travel in Germany. He had always hated the cold, and the chill was merciless then; his bones still ached from the frostbite of Afghanistan. All he had wanted to do was to stay indoors. But Atta had other plans.

Jarrah, Atta and Marwan checked into a small tradesmen's hotel in Munich's Obersendling district. The room had two beds, a single and a king-size. As soon as he had gotten the door open, Atta raced into the room. Hanging back in the hallway, Marwan reached into his pocket and pulled out a one-Euro coin. "Okay, I will flip you, Jarrah. The loser sleeps with Atta."

Jarrah chuckled. "Don't bother. Look what's going on." He pointed inside the doorway. They walked into the foyer. Atta was in the bathroom, his suitcase unzipped and spread apart on top of the single bed. "Did you bring your teddy bear?" Jarrah was giggling. "Because I don't want you hugging me in the middle of the night!"

They bundled up in parkas in the late afternoon to act like tourists taking a stroll through the town. Marwan had no idea why they had come. He was waiting for something to happen. But he was not sure he would recognize it when it did.

As they were heading out the door, Atta brought them up short. "Give me your passports," he demanded – in a condescending way. After two months of close-quarters living, his manner was wearing at Marwan. He knew that was just the way Atta was, and Atta did not mean anything by it, but Marwan wanted – as much as possible – to enjoy himself in Munich, since he could expect little pleasure for the remainder of his days.

"Are you giving me orders now?"

Atta turned from the door to the room and faced Marwan down. "Blood or no blood, Marwan, you do what I tell you to do. As I do what I am told to."

Jarrah shrugged. "Well, he's the boss." Marwan handed the papers over. Atta put them, with Jarrah's and his own, into an oversized wallet.

They walked all through the Altstadt – the Old City of Munich: past the Isartor, the Platzl, the Chamber Pot Museum; all around the Marienplatz and down Neuhauserstrasse. Just as they reached the Karlstor, Atta stopped dead in his tracks and began feeling in all of his pockets frantically.

"My God! They have stolen our passports!" He sounded desperate.

Marwan could not believe they had been stolen. On all the streets they had wandered down, no one had come within five feet of any one of them. The people of Munich were glum and rude. They had steered away from the Arabs. Now, when the Arabs were making a scene, the honest burghers of München slid even further aside.

"You lost our passports!" Marwan shouted.

"Lost, stolen, who knows, they are gone!"

"How could you be so sloppy?"

"Marwan, you're a moron," Jarrah cut in.

"What do you mean, a moron?!"

"Think, Marwan, for Allah's sake!" Atta hissed, hugging Marwan roughly from behind to put his mouth to his ear. "There are certain stamps in your passport that Americans should not see."

Islam is submission. And Marwan *was* a fool.

As they marched to the police station to report the theft, Jarrah had his head cocked, as if he were listening hard.

"What's up, Jarrah?" Marwan said, humbled now.

"I am trying to feel Hitler. He is in the air."

They stopped in a mosque for the evening prayers. Marwan waited for someone to contact them – a tap on the shoulder, maybe, or a whisper passing by. Nobody approached them.

They walked back to the hotel.

Outside the door, he held Jarrah back, let Atta get ahead. "Want to give Atta a heart attack? Let's take off all our clothes." He felt frisky. It must have been the cold.

Jarrah laughed, but he shook his head "no." "You keep your undies on."

They observed the salat, took off jackets and shoes and climbed into bed. Atta flipped on his bedside lamp. He lay on top of the covers and reached for his Qur'an.

"Night-night, Jarrah," Marwan said.

"Night-night, Marwan."

"Night-night, Atta," they both said.

Atta grumped: "Night-night."

# 21

**Delray Beach, Florida: June, 2001**

---

The new men were sleeping on the floor in Jarrah's flat, and in ours. There were seven of them, all Saudi, from the southwest of the peninsula, across the border from Yemen – from Al Baha, Abha, Khamis Mushayt, all the small 'Asir province towns that bracelet Highway 15, the road Sheikh Usama's father built which rises out of Mecca to serve Prince Khalid's new resorts in southwestern Arabia.

Thirty years ago, 'Asir was a primitive world, two millennia behind, wild as in Bedu history, tribal, cruel and remorseless, the land and the people both. It would take three days to go fifty miles, even if you had a car, which, once you left the city, you pushed more than you drove. Most people had only donkeys. No electricity. Modernity was barely comprehended there.

And then the prince – the governor, the falconer, the poet – built palaces and amusement parks (and, to be fair, schools, hospitals, airfields, electric lines, telephones) to bring 'Asir some of the oil wealth that otherwise hangs around Jeddah and Riyadh. And the rich came to the prince's resorts, because there is a cool breeze that blows through the mountains in summer.

But no Saudi will take a service job, and that is all there are in 'Asir – waiters, housekeepers, dishwashers, poolboys, prostitutes. So the boys of 'Asir have studied at the schools the princes built, but they have no work, and have no way to use anything they have learned. They see things on TV now, and read the newspapers, and listen to the imams who preach in the local mosques. They know what is going on in the world, and they hate the House of Saud, and Israel, and America, and all the Western world because they have nothing but empty pockets and fruitless plans.

If the Saudi royals are brought down, they have no one to blame but themselves. They are the ones who for years have preached the teachings of Taki ed-Din Ibn Taymiyyah who had said, seven hundred years ago, that the truth, and the rules for a proper life, were only to be found in the Qur'an (Allah's own words), the Sunnah (the written record of the Prophet's words and deeds) and commentaries from the time of the al-Salaf al-Salih, when Islam was ruled by the first three caliphs who followed the death of the Prophet. These rules are not to be interpreted; they are to be taken literally. They are to be obeyed completely, and not any other law. Anyone who fails in this is an unbeliever, the enemy of Allah, and Allah calls upon Muslims to shed his blood.

And it is not just in their own country that they have spread those beliefs. They funded Sheikh Usama. They funded the Taliban. They have spent billions founding madrassas in nearly every country around the world, including the U.S. The madrassas have created people like us, who think like Sheikh Usama – the kind of people madrassas were intended to create. The mistake the Saudi royals have made is failing to rule or to live by the principles they teach. So if the people they have taught turn their own doctrine against them, they will only have been hoisted by their own petard.

Our Saudis had been eager to sign up with Sheikh Usama. Many had been recruited by the imams who led their prayers, then sent to Peshawar and then to the Al Farouk camp in Afghanistan, near Khost, where they learned the less sophisticated ways to terminate a life. Some had been fighting the Russians in Chechnya. They had been hand-picked for our mission, returned to Kandahar and trained with a bit of English and a bit about flying planes. They knew where they were going, and they knew they were going to die. They did not know how and where it would be, but they knew why.

It was not by chance they had been chosen. Sheikh Usama wanted Saudis. It was a message to the royals, the same one he had been sending since Arabia had disowned him – that the Saudi people were with him, that he could bring the royals down. The royals were glad to pay him off in return for his commitment to leave them alone – for now. He was smart, Sheikh Usama – he told these recruits about his father who loved 'Asir, came out of 'Asir himself as an illiterate peasant and died a multibillionaire when his small plane fell out of the sky onto Highway 15. A poetic life, a poetic death. Very Arabian. And Sheikh Usama assured them that *he* loved the people, too. They believed it – and I thought it was most probably true.

Our Saudis were quiet, earnest, devoted to Islam, perhaps a little gullible, taciturn like all Bedu – but they made a racket at prayer time, and sometimes there were flare-ups when honor was at stake. These did not amount to anything, but things got thrown and voices got harsh and the walls of these Florida shacks were as porous as grapefruit pulp. The neighbors, with so many Arabs around, were beginning to get curious. They gave us that squinched-up look that said: Hey, you can stay here if you want, but we think you Ay-rabs live like pigs and never clean yourselves.

Their curiosity was dangerous. It was time to leave Hollywood. Atta sent me northward up Interstate 95 to find new rooms for the Saudis, scattered in different locations, as the manual requires. Some of the Saudis came along for the ride. We drove past Fort Lauderdale (too expensive) and Boca Raton (too many Jews). We got off the highway in Delray Beach, on Atlantic Avenue, and headed east toward the ocean, just looking around.

Now *here* was a gentrification which was working out – fancy new restaurants everywhere, antique shops packed with heirlooms carried south by now-dead New Yorkers, shops that sold incense and smooth stones and masks from Africa. There were private homes along the beach as huge as sultans' palaces, set off from the coast road A1A by huge trees trimmed into topiaries, banks of flowers and greenery and high stucco walls with massive gates. Plenty of Jews, but quieter and not as aggravating. To the Saudis, none of it mattered. But, as I considered it, if we had to be in Florida, why not here?

The Saudis and I went back west a ways and found a real estate office. The agent was a woman loaded with gold and diamonds; her hair was unbearably blonde, her face, arms and legs the color of roasted coffee beans. She had to be upwards of sixty, but she had dressed herself in a bright pink suit with the skirt to the top of her thighs. Her face had been pinned up more than once, and her breasts seemed locked in place, but her legs were still good, so she showed them, and I appreciated that. Of course, she was a Jewess. But I could be comfortable with Jews when I had to be.

I wanted two apartments, I said – one for my friends, one for me. My friends were in school, I told her, and needed a place for two months. I was in town to work with computers and would be here for three.

"Where do you live now?" she asked.

I said: "Nowhere. I'm wandering."

"So?" She was coy. "Are you busy tonight?"

I flinched. Just the thought of it. "Sorry, darling, I am."

In a yellow Mercedes convertible, she led us to a place called the Delray Racquet Club. The available apartment was on the fifth floor of Building One, a pumpkin-colored construction in the Mizner style, like everything they are building in Palm Beach County now. They call it Mediterranean, but it is bastardized Tuscan and Provençal and Moorish and whatever else. The people who owned the apartment spent their summers in Colorado. The landscaping was lovely. The Saudis did not care.

"This is the home of the Rod Laver Tennis Academy." The pink lady pointed to tennis courts I could not see. "They get lots of foreigners, from all over the world. Lots of folks for people like you to make friends with." It was nine hundred dollars a month. I said I would take it.

Next we saw an apartment at the Hamlet Country Club. Most of western Palm Beach County lives like this – small houses around a golf course or lake, behind guarded walls. The next day, two Saudis moved into each of the places I had found.

Atta did not like the three Saudis I still had to find a home for – he thought they were too bigheaded and did not give him the proper respect, and he had told me not to put them in the lap of luxury. Quality of life erodes going up Route One north of Delray, but you pass by the Homing Inn before it is entirely gone. There were four three-story buildings. There were no elevators. The room I rented was on the third floor – one double, one twin – free HBO and a microwave and banged-up cooking utensils.

The Saudis already knew everything they needed to know for now, and their only instructions were to lay low and keep fit. They were not to go to the areas where the Muslims lived, because we did not know what the Saudis might say, or whether the green-card Arabs were with us or were not. So, because their English was so parenthetical, the Saudis lacked all human contact. They stayed away from the swimming pools, because they could not expose their bodies or look at the bikini-waxed women lolling there. Their own naked shaved faces were blasphemy enough. They were taken for rude by their neighbors – and they might have been rude if they could have been, but one can't be rude when one can't communicate at all.

The men I stored at the Homing Inn refused to let in the housemaids, and they would not do women's work, so the room went filthy fast. They had no cars and couldn't read the routes of the buses, so they stayed pinned to their quarters, where we wanted them to be. They passed the days sitting in the doorway to their room. They were horribly homesick. Sometimes they cried. They were kids, most of them.

They did not use their kitchen – again, women's work. Somehow they ordered Chinese food, or picked up a box of donuts. They were crazy about the donuts – just like Atta was.

Finally Atta and I took pity on them and introduced them to Denny's, down Route One south of the Homing Inn. We would take them there at eleven p.m., when the place was empty. I chatted up the waitresses, Michelle and her mother Donna, and taught them what the Saudis liked – coffee, orange juice, steak, and vegetable omelets. The Saudis learned to say thank you, but I overheard Donna say one night that they had not learned to tip.

They signed up at gyms, and walked to them. No one does weights in Arabia; the exercise lacks finesse. They banged the machines, staggered around, but they kept at it religiously – no intent to pun. They did not drop a barbell on anyone's toes, and the mats came in handy when prayers had to be said. Atta, on the other hand, was pumping for all he was worth. "You ought to try it," he told me. "You are getting a little too pudgy."

The Saudis got Florida licenses or Florida I.D.'s. They used them to open bank accounts, one or two of them to a branch, to avoid undue attention. They walked to internet cafés or public libraries, and used email to keep in touch with their families. If back home there was no computer, they rented a post office box. No Arab son cuts his family off unless he is up to no good. I did not write to my mother. She didn't know where I was.

And over and over, they would ask us: "Emta?" When? We did not know the answer; if we had, we would not have told them. We didn't want more edge on them than there already was. Their eagerness impressed me. I wished I could be as keen.

When it came time for Atta and me to move, Atta would not let me choose a new home for the two of us. He had had Saudis sleeping on his floor; now he wanted his own space, and so did I. We took adjoining apartments in a pleasant white condominium in Coral Springs, just west of Pompano Beach. That was the first time Atta let me spend any time alone.

Jarrah found a one-bedroom flat in the rear of a modest one-story gray house, three blocks from the ocean in Lauderdale-By-The-Sea. A wind chime with a sign that read: "This House Is Full Of Love" twirled over the front door. Jarrah used a side entrance, and never noticed it.

# 22

---

Bad Teeth removed his shoes at the door to Atta's flat. Which was now Marwan's flat as well – Bahaji had moved out as promised, and Marwan had his room. Bad Teeth was not in a suit this time, just a light blue cashmere sweater and khaki Docker pants.

"I have a paper for you to sign."

"Come in," Marwan said.

"Is Atta here?"

"No. He's at work."

"At work? What work? Where does he work? I thought he was through with such things."

"He works at the plant that makes the Airbus 300 airplane."

Bad Teeth sighed and threw up his hands. "What is he doing there?"

"Cleaning the planes."

"Ah," he smiled. It was ugly. "I understand. So, when it happens, he will know where the cockpit is. Tell him for that he can quit his job. It is usually in front. May I sit?"

Marwan showed him to the dining table, pulled out a chair for him. Bad Teeth withdrew a printed form from his jacket pocket.

"What is it?" Marwan asked.

"You have an account at the Dresdner Bank?"

"Yes …"

"Into which certain people are making certain deposits? This paper is called a power of attorney. It will let me control that bank account. So I can send money to you. With this I can sign your name. They will think you are still in Hamburg."

"Does Atta know?"

"Of course he does."

"Shouldn't I ask him first?"

Bad Teeth frowned. "If you wish." He began to pull the paper away. But Marwan signed it. It made sense.

Bad Teeth stood, walked toward the doorway. "I wish I were going with you," he said. And Marwan wanted to strangle him. Some of the people who told him that meant what they said. But Bad Teeth? Would he have jumped at the chance to do what Marwan was going to do?

"Why don't you take my place?" Marwan said. Bad Teeth blanched. He would not have done it. "It's not too late."

Bad Teeth came and rested his delicate fingers lightly on Marwan's shoulders. "You are my hero," he said. "All our hearts are with you."

Marwan looked up at him vacantly. "I hope, where we go, it's warm."

# 23

**Boston; Las Vegas: July, 2001**

---

"Delta would like to be the first to welcome you to Boston." The stewardess modulated her voice; I had heard her talk to a steward, and her real tone was high and sharp. I didn't understand. How could she welcome me to Boston if she was on the same plane? Didn't she have to get there first so she could welcome me? Or if not, why couldn't I be the first to welcome *her* to Boston?

Atta and I stayed that night in a hotel close to Logan Airport. In the morning the hotel's minivan dropped us at Logan Departures. We had chosen the two Boston flights for the Day: one from American Airlines, the other from United. American flew out of Terminal B; United used Terminal C. Atta got off at the first of these. I got off at the second.

I verified curbside check-in, which we planned to use. Security had no problem letting me down to the gates. I told

171

them I was meeting a friend; they did not think twice about it. I noticed the food court and the shops; if we got to the airport early, we planned to scatter the Saudis into these shops to keep them apart from each other and away from security cameras. I spotted all of the cameras, and noted their locations. The staff at the gates – they were mostly girls – did not seem well-trained. Still, we would not want to do anything that would get their hackles up.

I met Atta back at the hotel about an hour later. Atta said: "No problem." I agreed.

I don't know why, but I felt nothing that morning – no exultation, no fear, no despair. I would be flying to death from this airport – yet it was as if the place had no significance. Perhaps feelings were dangerous. That must be it.

When we returned the following day, we tested the check-in procedures. United took my luggage and gave me a boarding pass. I answered the two stupid questions: yes, I packed my bags myself, and no, my bags have not been out of my possession. I am a professional terrorist. I am much too careful for that.

We had read on the internet that passengers could bring aboard knives that had less than a four-inch blade. I had packed one of those Swiss Army knives in my carry-on. The bag went under the xray. Nobody said a thing. I meandered as casually as I could down to the gate, looking up at the cameras so they would catch my face. I was daring them to figure me out – but it would seem they did not.

When they called the flight, I boarded it. Boston-Chicago-Las Vegas. Time for another meeting with the West Coast cell.

In Las Vegas this time, Atta chose the Econo Lodge, a two-building, two-story, one-diamond place described on the internet as "basic accommodation." It was on Las Vegas Boulevard, but twelve blocks north of downtown and nine blocks south of the Strip; i.e., in the middle of nowhere, with no temptations at hand except for the "Home of the Five Dollar Lap Dance" next door.

The cast of characters was the same as on our last trip to Las Vegas, except that Jarrah had come this time. When they were all gathered in our room, al-Midhar was in the mood to get quickly to the point.

"Your people have come?" he asked Atta.

"Yes."

"How many?

"Seven."

Al-Midhar frowned. "Not enough. And we have only six."

There were footsteps in the hallway, and then a knock at the door. Jarrah jumped to behind the door. Al-Midhar went into his pocket and brought out a throwing knife. Al-Hazmi whipped out a deck of cards and scattered them on a table.

"Sorry," I laughed. "I forgot. I ordered pizzas from Domino's."

Jarrah heaved the door open. There was a man in the

hallway with a square red bag. Two extra cheese thin-crusts came out of it. Al-Hazmi gathered up his cards, and they and al-Midhar's weapon went back into their pockets. They all ate the pizzas, even though they hated me.

Atta impatiently picked up the thread. "We have six pilots, all of us here, seven if we get Moussaoui. But in total only nineteen men, or twenty with Moussaoui. That is only enough to take four planes.

It was al-Hazmi who answered him. "So that is how many we take."

"We have five targets."

"We leave one out. One in Washington. That will be for al-Midhar and me to decide."

Atta nodded. "All right. So we do not need Moussaoui."

Cheese and tomato sauce tumbled off al-Hazmi's slice. "Damn it!" he growled. "I forgot to bring another shirt." He ran into the kitchen and turned the faucet on.

Al-Midhar answered Atta. "We do not need him as a pilot. But remember we are still one short of five men for each plane. Moussaoui is in Pakistan. Al-Shibh and the commander met him. They think he has got a big mouth and a big sense of himself. They don't want to use him, except as a last resort. But they are sending him back to America, to another flying school – I suppose in case something happens to one of us."

"Something like what?" asked Atta.

"Like somebody changing his mind." Al-Midhar shot a

sidelong glance at me.

"That will never happen," Atta said.

"Let us hope not. By the way, we have decided not to take two planes in Newark."

Atta raised his eyebrows. "What are you talking about?"

"If you want to take two out of Boston, that is your business. But I will not do that in Newark. Two groups of five Arabs on flights to California leaving five minutes apart? Americans are not stupid. That is too much of a chance."

For Atta, it had just been confirmed that he was not controlling these events as he had thought he would. "All right," he surrendered. "What are you going to do?"

"We take a plane in Washington. At Dulles International."

"And it hits what?"

"What does it matter?"

"Of course it matters! By the time you take over the plane, it will be miles from Washington."

"So," al-Midhar shrugged, "we will turn it around."

"Or else," al-Hazmi suggested, "we could take it to New York." His wet shirt now looked as if he had been shot in the heart.

"Marwan and I will go to New York." Atta's tone was deadly.

"All right!" Al-Hazmi threw up his hands. "Any way you want it. But we want Jarrah to fly one of our planes."

"What do you want him for?"

"We need another pilot."

"You have three already."

Al-Midhar took over the point. "Al-Hazmi and me, to be honest, we can't fly those planes. Jarrah flies one, Hanjour flies the other. We stay in the cabin. We are better at what has to be done in the back of the plane."

Jarrah joined the palaver, addressing himself to Atta. "I met them in Vegas last month. I have agreed to this."

"Jarrah can go to Newark," al-Midhar said. "Al-Hazmi and me and Hanjour will go to Washington. Jarrah can pick what target he wants. Then we will pick ours."

Atta nodded to al-Midhar. The matter was resolved. "But … " Atta snatched at al-Midhar's sleeve. "I want to meet your Saudis." If Atta were going to lose control, it would not be without a fight.

Al-Midhar plucked Atta's fingers off his shirt. "So make a stop in New Jersey on your way home from here."

# 24

**Hamburg: May, 2000**

---

Bahaji's new flat was miniscule: two small, dark first-floor rooms, almost windowless, not far from the apartment house where Bad Teeth and his Byelorussian wife had an equally tiny place. Marwan had come to say good bye. It was the first step he had taken that had really sunk home in him. "Goodbye" no longer meant to him what it always had.

"I couldn't do it, Marwan," Bahaji said, with complete dejection, as they sat across from each other in two huge loungers that took up most of the room.

"Then it's good that you aren't going to."

"But someday they will ask something like it of me."

"You can refuse …"

"And for the rest of my miserable life not be able to look anyone in the eye." Bahaji straightened up slightly from his slump, to engage Marwan's gaze. "How will you make yourself do it? Al-Shibh wants to go to Paradise. I think that is because he

177

has never in his life gotten laid. Or had any creature comforts. Or any respect from anyone. He will get all of that in Paradise. But you – you have a good life. Why do you want to end it?"

The question was meaningless. Marwan did not *want* to die.

"I don't buy that intolerant bullshit, that Taliban misery." Bahaji became more frenetic with every word. "I am German-born, remember, not a fucking Saudi. My family comes from Morocco, where Islam is sweet and there are other things to think about in this life besides Allah. The thought of killing someone does not exalt me, either. And I don't hate America. Or what it makes, or what it believes. If it were not for America, the world would be asleep. What I hate is things America does – especially to us."

Marwan nodded. "And they must be punished for those …"

"Jihad, yes! It must be done!" Bahaji thumped his fists on his thighs. "But there are many ways to do it without killing yourself on purpose!"

Not for me, Marwan thought.

He had only once let himself think about whether, if he had asked for it, they would have assigned him to something he had a chance to survive. But if it had not been for Atta, they would not have bothered with him. So, for him, it was all or nothing. He understood.

"My wife is pregnant," Bahaji said. His thumb flipped over his shoulder, toward another room. That was where she was hiding. No one could look at her.

Marwan stood, went over and hugged him, and let himself out.

# 25

**Paterson, New Jersey: July, 2001**

---

I t was a *jämmerlich* building in a town that was full of them,
completely covered, inside and out, with that strange
calligraphy American blacks use to mark their territory. The
hallways smelled of ancient piss, and the wooden floors looked
like leopard skin, scarred by hundreds of cigarette butts ground
out under heels. The mailboxes were bent and the locks were
gone, pried out long ago, no doubt in the course of the theft
of welfare checks.

The three-room apartment – no furniture – was over a
*bodega*. There was beer in the refrigerator for al-Midhar and
al-Hazmi – Hanjour said he liked the taste, but he mixed the
beer with water so it did not intoxicate. But none of the three
of them actually dwelt in Paterson, New Jersey. They flew in
from San Diego every once in a while. Only their Saudis lived
in the place, left on their own hook. They were as helpless

as ours had been, trying to keep themselves alive on Chinese food and donuts and sleeping on a crack house floor, from the looks of it.

These Saudis did not interest me any more than ours. But within ten minutes of walking in, Atta had fixed on one of them, an open-faced boy with wide-spaced eyes and heavy lips so sensual he looked like a girl. He called himself al-Omari. That was not his name. The passport he was traveling on had been stolen several years before from a Saudi pilot in Denver.

When we all went for dinner that night to the Wo Ting China Emporium – where the window curtains were greasy bamboo and the floor shone with ground-in lo mein and crawled with well-fed roaches – al-Omari's and Atta's rickety chairs were practically on top of each other. They shared their food, their eyes were locked and whatever it was they had to say was for themselves alone.

It was not sexual. For Arabs, this sort of feeling was not uncommon between two men. But it was not common for it to strike like love at first sight. I was jealous of al-Omari. I had known Atta how long? Without one intimate moment.

Two could play at that game, at least as far as appearances went, excluding the sentiment. Hanjour was sitting by himself, looking miserable. I noisily scraped my chair back from the common table, moved over to Hanjour and put my chair next to his.

It was painful to get him to talk to me. Like Sheikh Usama,

he would not meet your gaze – but when I finally caught his wet eyes I saw no spark, and I knew he was not a mujihad, just a boy too suggestible for his own good.

"You don't seem the type to be doing this."

He looked up with a wan smile. "No? Neither do you."

"How did they get you into it?"

"Al-Midhar saw me at flying school."

"You wanted to be a pilot?"

"Since I was a little boy."

In the early '90's, he told me, his older brother Abdulrahman – who was a drinker and a partier, not religious as Hani was – used to go to the United States to buy up "pre-owned" Cadillacs to resell in Arabia. To get things started for Hani, he had taken him along and, through Saudi friends in Tucson, had enrolled him in an English course at the University of Arizona. But the language had daunted Hani; he could not get hold of it. After three months of frustration and fear, he had gone home to Saudi Arabia, where he managed his family's lemon farm in Taif, in 'Asir province.

He had tried America again in 1996. This time, he had gone to Florida and stayed in the town of Miramar with Arabs whom his brother had met years before in Tucson. He lasted a month in Miramar. His hosts told his brother that they had not seen much of him. He told me that in Miramar he had never brushed his teeth, because he had forgotten to bring a toothbrush and hadn't the nerve to ask his hosts if he could borrow one.

But, gathering up his courage, he had left Florida on his own and gone to California, because he had heard about a flying school out there, in San Diego. He did not do well at the school, he said. It was not that he couldn't grasp how to fly a plane – he just could not understand what he was told by anyone speaking English.

He had moved to Phoenix after that, tried another flying school. He had not had any better success. But his English was improving with the passage of time, and he had finally passed the flight exam back at the San Diego school. That was when al-Hazmi and al-Midhar had recruited him. He told me that in San Diego they had called those two "Dumb and Dumber." They were the worst pilots the school had ever seen.

He had applied for a flying job with Saudia Airlines. He had gotten no response. So now he was going to glory with Bin Laden Air. I guess, one way or the other, we all get what we want.

I liked Hanjour. I was not pretending to when Atta asked me to come with him; he wanted to get some flying time close to New York City, to have a first-hand look at the targets from the air. I said I would go up, but not with him. I wanted to fly with Hanjour. Now Atta was envious, I was pleased to see.

Hanjour and I followed after him and al-Omari as they flew toward the tip of Manhattan, fifteen miles southeast. But we turned back at the Hudson, and let Atta go on alone. That was as much of Manhattan as I was ready for.

# 26

## Costa Dorada, Spain: July, 2001

A tta deplaned at Barajas International Airport near Madrid. He had to wait five hours there until my flight came in. We spent the night under false names at a hotel near the airport. The next morning we rented a car and drove northeast to the outskirts of Barcelona, and then south along the Costa Dorada to Tarragona. We checked into the Hotel Sant Jordi, on the Via Augusta. It was a short walk from there to the shore of the Mediterranean. That night, I stood on the beach and stared out into the sea. Home was out there somewhere. I would not see it again.

In the morning, an SUV arrived and took us to an expensive home somewhere in Tarragona. Abu Dahdah let us in. His wife and kids were not there. In the living room, we found Jarrah, Bahaji and al-Shibh, and Abu Ilyas from Hamburg who exported TVs, and the same three suits from Aleppo we had seen before in Madrid. There was also an Algerian, whose house, I guess, we were in, since anything anyone put down, the Algerian picked up.

Al-Shibh was as warm as he could be, which was anyone else's tepid. The Syrians were cordial, but the air was full of imminence, which damped conviviality. Only Bahaji and Jarrah showed any emotion at all. I got short hugs from both of them. Then it was down to business.

None of us had the courage to have this discourse sitting down. We all paced the living room, circling each other.

"Are you ready?" Abu Dahdah began.

Atta asked about Moussaoui.

"Forget about him, he is *nutzlos*," said al-Shibh, "You already know that." He said Moussaoui was going to go to another flying school, this time in Minnesota. But there would no longer be time to get him up to speed. "You have chosen the flights?" he asked Atta.

"Yes."

"Tell me what they are."

"Marwan will take United Airlines Flight 175. It leaves Boston for Los Angeles at 8:15 in the morning. His target will be the south tower, in New York. Mine is American Airlines Flight 11. It leaves Boston at 7:55, also for Los Angeles. We will hit the north tower. Both flights will be using 767's. Jarrah gets United Flight 93, going to San Francisco. It leaves Newark at 8:42. The others will be on American Flight 77, it leaves at 8:10 for Los Angeles from Dulles International. Those flights are using 757's. Jarrah has chosen to hit the Capitol. Hanjour's plane will turn around and blow up the Pentagon."

"So we have no plane for President Bush."

"Not this time."

"You have done the calculations?"

"Of course. What do you think?"

"You will all hit your targets simultaneously?"

"If things go as I have planned them," Atta explained, "if we capture the planes quickly, and turn them in the right place, Marwan and I will hit the towers at about the same time. The other two will have to work things out for themselves. Anything can happen. It is in the hands of Allah."

Al-Shibh and Atta locked eyes. Then al-Shibh nodded. "Have you picked the day?"

Atta promised to have it for him soon.

"I must tell Sheikh Usama …"

"I said *soon*!"

"Don't be short with me, brother!" al-Shibh snapped. "We are all in expectance, not just you."

"Sorry," Atta apologized bitterly. "I do the best I can."

Abu Dahdah spoke soothingly. "Yes, we know. We trust you. It will be fine."

"Three things more," al-Shibh went on. "You will go to Las Vegas again, all the pilots will meet for the final niceties. We are going to send a man there to help you with the details of how you have to go about taking the planes.

"Also, we are discussing another operation – not for any of you, of course. We are thinking of using crop-dusting planes to spread chemicals and diseases. There are many crop-dusters in Florida. We want you to talk to some of them, maybe fly one of their airplanes, find out how it is done."

"Okay," Atta said. "I will take care of it."

"For the last thing, Sheikh Usama insists: Once you have taken a plane, if for any reason it appears you are going to fail, you *must* crash the aircraft rather than let yourselves be captured. All of you … do you understand?"

The corners of Jarrah's mouth turned up, though he knew this was no time to smile. "We are not exactly idiots."

Al-Shibh shouted: "Do you agree?!!"

I did not seem able to speak when the others answered him.

"I am sorry," Abu Dahdah cut in, "but one more point. If at the end any of you has any money left, you will send it back to us. We will need it for other things. You will wire it to a friend in the Emirates whose name we will give you then."

We all shook hands solemnly, the grips tight and strong. I saw al-Shibh go to Atta and whisper in his ear. Then al-Shibh came to me; unexpectedly, he drew me in and hugged me to his chest. "I wish I were dying with you," he sobbed.

I lay my hand on his shoulder blade and softly patted him. "I would gladly have given you my place. Don't worry – insh'Allah, some day you will get your chance."

We were on the Costa Dorada, the summer weather was beautiful, and Jarrah, Bahaji, Atta and I were together again. We had been working hard on the job for thirteen months. I wanted a vacation, like normal people had.

Jarrah and Bahaji jumped at the chance. Atta had to be convinced. We spent the night in Tarragona; the next day, we headed south down the coastal road. We stopped in Reus in the afternoon to see the modernist architecture. The town was famous for it. The style did not look modern to me; it reminded me of pictures I had seen of the great French Riviera resorts at the turn of the century. Atta didn't like the design; it was too decadent.

It was twilight when we reached Salou. Atta and I checked us in at the Casablanca Playa. It was white, seven stories tall, very Floridian, one of a hundred small hotels and condos which overlooked the beach. The desk clerk insisted on cash in advance. Sorry, he said, palming the bills – but these Arab and African immigrants run out in the morning without settling their accounts ... and Salou was very busy, we were lucky to get a room ...

That night, Jarrah, Bahaji and I went out to walk the beach. Germans and Brits were everywhere – fat, underdressed and noisy. The whole town stank of Coppertone. Pools of vomit dotted the sand; Led Zeppelin songs and fist fights spilled out of the waterfront bars along Av. Jaume I. Tattooed snakes crawled up girls' backs from out of bikini bottoms. People were fucking in doorways. Women whipped off their shirts. The place was *geschmacklos, unterklasse*, and I was delighted with it.

We had dinner at a restaurant on Av. Carles Buigas, took the risk of sitting together, ordered drinks we did not touch. Danced to Michael Jackson in basement discotheques. Parceled out three women who had a penthouse suite; rampaged between their legs, gave them a goodbye kiss. Scoured the gutters at four a.m., picking up empty bottles and cigarette butts to dump into the trash cans when we got back to our rooms, because neatness and sobriety were conspicuous in Salou.

Atta was still up when I got back, reading the Qur'an. "Thanks for letting us do this," I said.

"Oh, you're welcome," he yawned. "Don't ask again."

"I don't really like Hanjour better than you."

"Of course not. How could you? Hanjour is a nincompoop."

It was nearly noon when I awoke the next day. Atta was dressed and gone. I had breakfast alone on our balcony – cinnamon toast, scrambled eggs and Israeli oranges. Jarrah came to get me. Bahaji was still asleep. I pulled on a pair of bathing trunks and we went out, found a few feet of unoccupied sand and spent the afternoon sucking oysters out of their shells and staring at perky man-made tits and the greasy guys running after them.

Atta had taken the car and driven south on the Costa Blanca, beyond Valencia to Alicante. He described that town for me later: a city on mountains beside the sea, built by the Moors on Roman ruins a thousand years ago. The Spanish had recaptured the town from the Moors in 1246, but there was still visible evidence of Islam's great days. The sight of Alicante, and what had become of it – the decadence and debauchery he could not help but despise in the restaurants and discos along the Esplanada – made him think with joy of the reason that he was going to die.

# 27

**Belle Glade, Florida: July, 2001**

---

There were miles and miles of sugar cane fields, and nothing else, driving west out Southern Boulevard on the long, flat, straight road that led to Lake Okeechobee. Thirty miles inland, the Palm Beaches peter out. It is cracker country out there – sugar, cattle ranches – until on the banks of the great lake were Pahokee, Cardwell, Runyon, Belle Glade, farm worker communities, seedy, peeling and poor.

Belle Glade was full of prisons and trailer parks, and houses not much bigger than a doublewide. Tiny airstrips were scattered on patches of grass around the town. On one of these sat a stubby blue and yellow plane. A black man on a ladder was giving the engine a tune. We parked our car on the edge of the field and sauntered over to him.

"Howdy," he said.

We said "howdy".

"Whut kin I do fo' y'all?"

"Well," I said, "we're pilots, y'see …"

His yellow eyes were lowering. "Oh, now, that ain't good."

"It ain't? Why not?"

He tapped his wrench on the cowling, then put it down. "You Palestinians done opened those department stores ovuh on Avenue A, run all the coluhed stores outta town. Robbed the coluhed blind. I thought we had got rid a y'all when the farm machines came in and wiped out all that migrant work, emptied out this town, took away yo' bidness. Now you want to come back and move in on *me*? I been out hyah thirty years. What you want to do that fo'?"

"We're not Palestinians."

"You look like you is."

"No, we're from … Algeria."

"Ain't that in that there Middle East?" I had to admit it sort of was. "Sheeit, you Palestinians, then. You gonna dust 'roun' hyah?"

"Look, we were just driving around and saw your plane. We are not going to cropdust anywhere. Just a couple of questions. You know, pilot-to-pilot stuff, things you know that we don't. Like, what kind of plane is this?"

"Air Tractor 502."

Atta cut in. "How much fuel does it hold?"

The black answered cautiously. "Wall, 'bout three hours worth."

"And how much pesticide?"

"Five hunnert gallons. Do a field or two."

At that, Atta grabbed onto a wing and pulled himself up toward the cockpit. The black man snatched at his ankles. "Hey, you get offa they!"

"I just want to sit in the plane …" Atta said.

"Well, you cain't. Now get the hell down." He pulled Atta off the wing.

Atta's upper lip curled. "Don't you touch me again!"

"Then stay offa my machine."

"Well, would you mind," I asked him, "if we hung out and watched you fly her?"

"Yes, I mind. Ain't no work right now. You wait til I fly this plane, you be *hangin'* for a week!" He picked up the wrench and waggled it. "Now listen up, y'all, I am jes' a little *busy* …"

# 28

**Las Vegas: August, 2001**

---

"We learned nothing about the cropdusters," Atta said. "We tried." The West Coasters nodded. But that had nothing to do with them. We were back in Vegas, at the Econo Lodge again. The temperature climbed past 104. We stayed inside.

The man al-Shibh had told us would come was in his thirties, slim. He had a can of beer in one hand and a lit cigarette in the other. He grabbed up a battered barstool and centered it in the room, perched himself upon it and waved us to come in close. Hanjour sidled next to me. "I know this man," he whispered. "He is a flight instructor in Phoenix. He was one of my teachers. We lived together a while."

"Looks like an American," I whispered back.

"No, he is Algerian. He has just been here too long."

A light smile played on the visitor's lips as he began to tell us the "niceties" we had not thought about yet.

"We want you to book one-way – no need to spend extra money, We already know one-way flights will not raise any red flags. Book your seats in two locations, some of you in first class, some of you further back. Only two locations – do not spread out further than that. Split the Saudis between the two. Anyone who is without the guts to slit a throat needs to be sitting next to somebody who will."

A quick shock struck at my heart. The remnants surged down my arms and legs, making the muscles twitch. I had brought myself to accept so much in the past year and a half; yet I had never made myself understand that there would have to be killing done before I killed myself – dirty killing, that I would have to watch, or maybe even do. There was a line drawn somewhere in my soul, and I was stepping over it. I despised brutality. It disgusted me.

"Some of you bring a boxcutter – one of those little retractable knives you can buy in a hardware store. Not all of you, that will look too weird. One of you on each plane brings aboard in his carry-on something that when you strap it on will look like a bomb – but will not look suspicious when they xray the bag. Like one of those safari vests, the ones with all the pockets. You can dye it black, rip it up and pad it out with cotton. But that really is not necessary. If you just say you have a bomb, they will believe you.

"Don't wait until the plane gets to cruising altitude. You need to make your move about twenty minutes into the flight.

Someone gets up and announces he has a bomb. There will be a lot of commotion. The rest of you have to move fast. Some of you push the passengers to the back of the plane. If the flight attendants give you trouble, shut them up. After that, whoever is in front opens the cockpit door.

"Tell the pilots no one is going to get hurt, say you want money, or you want the Israelis to let someone out of jail. They are trained to surrender the plane, to keep the passengers safe. If you can get them out of the cockpit, put them back with the passengers. Then sit down and take control of the plane. If they do not move out, or they put up a fight, slit their throats. If the passengers get physical, use your knives, or there is always an axe in the cockpit. Or you can cut off the oxygen to the passenger cabin. But if you do that, brothers, make sure you are all in the cockpit and the door is closed. What you want to do at that point is kill them, not yourselves."

Oh, this is *cold,* I thought. Why won't he shut up!

"Once you have control of the plane, turn off the transponder. You all have flight deck videos, you know where it is. That way, radar can track you but they will not know who you are. Then you talk to the passengers. Be sure you are using the internal PA and not a radio – otherwise air traffic control will hear everything you say. Tell the passengers there is a bomb, if you have not already; you have taken over the plane, you are going to turn back to the airport, stay calm …

"If you know enough to use the built-in navigation, do

it. If you do not, use a handheld GPS. Set in the target's coordinates; I've written them all down." He pulled a paper out of his pocket and waved it around. "Memorize them before you leave and burn this sheet.

"Atta, you make your turn over central Massachusetts, head for the New York border, you can follow the Hudson River down to New York City. For the two planes to hit close in time, Marwan will have to turn south further east; his plane leaves later, he will need a shorter route. Are you listening to me, Marwan?" Hanjour reached over and shook me.

"Atta and Marwan, come into your targets at around nine hundred feet. You want to fly fast, but not too fast. Keep under five hundred miles an hour. If you fly faster, you may do more damage, but the plane is not designed to fly at those speeds at low altitudes, you run the risk of it breaking up, particularly in a turn. Even I could not hold the pitch in a turn at that kind of speed, and I know how to fly these planes. With you, it is a guessing game. Also it looks suspicious. Below ten thousand feet, the FAA's speed limit is two hundred eighty seven.

"When you are about to hit your target, bank the wings. Not enough to start a turn, but enough to expand the area of the building that you hit. The more floors you impact, the more people die. The rest of you, going to Washington, come in as low as you can. Brush the ground with the belly. Hit straight on.

"Okay. Any questions?" he smiled. Nobody said a word.

He got up from the barstool and stubbed his cigarette out on the beer can. "Okay. Good luck. Sorry I can't stick around. My wife and kids are downstairs. I promised I would take them to the water park."

*I am in the cockpit, a hundred lights are blinking, air traffic control is screaming "Who are you?" The building is huge in front of me. People at the windows – bankers with their sleeves rolled up, secretaries in sneakers – staring out with huge eyes, they cannot comprehend it. My hand is on the throttle, holding it down …* "Wherever you are, death will find you out. Even if you are in towers built up strong and high."

*La ilaha il-lalahu halimul karim. La ilaha il-lalahu 'aliyyud 'azim .. I mean these words. I believe them.* "And surely the Hour will come in which there is no doubt. And the reckoning is the truth. The Paradise is the truth."

# 29

**Delray Beach, Florida: August, 2001**

---

Atta and I had just returned from Palm Beach County Park Airport, north of us, in Lantana, another flat Florida town. We had rented a Piper Archer, flown over the Everglades. Atta was parking in front of his flat when his cell phone rang. He answered it, and I saw the blood drain out of his cheeks.

He shut the phone down absently. "Moussaoui has been arrested."

"What?"

"The flight school got suspicious of him."

"*Yaha*," I said. Oh, shit.

"Al-Shibh had a man in Norman watching Moussaoui. He said the flight school people thought it was odd that Moussaoui didn't seem to care about taking off and landing. He did not know what Moussaoui had said to them, but he overheard the instructors talking among themselves about how much damage a Boeing could cause if it crashed into a building.

"They brought in the F.B.I. There were visa violations … They searched his room; they found manuals for the 747 and a little telephone notebook with al-Shibh's number in it. The Marienstraße apartment. They called al-Shibh. He did not pick up the phone."

I tried to put a good face on the disaster. "We were not going to use Moussaoui .."

"Marwan, please, you miss the point. He has put them onto al-Shibh."

"Al-Shibh won't tell them anything. You know that."

Atta sat down heavily in his only chair. "They can make the connection from him to us. They can find us, and they can find out what we have been doing here. That ought to convince them, if they have any doubts, that they have guessed the truth with Moussaoui. And if they get Moussaoui talking, they will *know* what is going on."

Atta put his head in his hands and pressed hard on the temples. "Well … Moussaoui is a dolt, but he's tough, and he's mean. He won't tell them anything. Even under torture …. But time is against us now." He began to look around the room, but he could not seem to focus. "Where are the airline schedules? Marwan, where did I put them? And we have a calendar, I think. Where is that?"

"I don't know …"

"*Help me, for Allah's sake!*"

So you are not all iron, I thought. That is good to know.

I went into Atta's bedroom. I knew he kept all his papers there, hidden from me. The room was impeccably tidy, as if it were in a five-star hotel and Atta had just checked in. Not a wrinkle in the bedcovers. Nothing of his in sight. In his dresser, his shirts and underwear were neatly folded and stacked (mine, once scooped out of the dryer, were thrown into a drawer. When I reached for a pair of underpants, everything came out.) In his closet, his few jackets and pants were hung by color and category. Mine were gathering lint in a corner of the floor.

I found his black duffle bag under his bed. I pulled it out, opened it and shuffled through its contents – flight deck videos; cockpit diagrams; aeronautical maps; all his books from the flight school; cans of Egyptian foods; a German-English dictionary; a Triple A Florida guide; manuals on kung fu, jiu jitsu and karate and a flyer from the World Gym in Boynton Beach; operational manuals for Boeing jets; passports from various countries under various names; three disposable cell phones; his GPS; books by Qutb and several Qur'ans, one clean, one marked up and written in; a white three ring binder with notes in Atta's hand; a pile of American dollars; flight schedules of every airline that flew out of Logan Airport; a tiny black notebook full of code keys and telephone numbers. The inside front page of the notebook was a current calendar.

I retrieved it and the schedules of American and United, re-zipped the duffel bag and shoved it back under the bed.

Atta was speeding like a mayfly, which has a lifetime's work to do in just one day. He snatched the documents out of my hand. He opened the telephone notebook and flipped to the calendar, then spread the schedules out on his lap and thumbed through them rapidly. He peered at the tiny printing. Then he slapped the schedules shut. He stared for another moment at the calendar. Then he closed the notebook carefully.

"Do you know what al-Shibh whispered to me when we were in Spain? It was the date Ramzi Yousef was convicted. September 11th. Five years ago." He tapped a thumb on the notebook. "Tuesday, September 11th. That is the Day."

# 30

**Deerfield Beach, Florida: August, 2001**

---

We moved our Saudis out of Delray, just as a precaution, because the longer they stayed in one place the more unfortunate inferences might be drawn. They were in a motel in Deerfield Beach, just below Boca Raton. Atta and I packed up and moved to the same motel. We had to be able to supervise every move they made.

The Panther was a small motel on the west side of A1A, a nondescript white building like so many others we had used, an L around a swimming pool with an indescribable shape. On the wall of the room we were given was a sepia photograph of a girl holding a parasol and wearing pantaloons – a 1920's bathing beauty, I supposed. Her shoulders and her legs below the knees were bare. Atta was halfway through the door when he caught sight of her. He dropped his bag, ran to the bathroom, snatched a towel off a rack and threw it over the picture. The duffel went under Atta's bed. I pretended I didn't see it.

The Saudis had been at loose ends for almost three months now. They had been doing their regular workouts; other than that, they had been sitting around their coffee cups, spinning Arabian fantasies which were doing them no good. Now they had work to do. We had to tighten them up.

Atta and I were sitting at a table in our room. He was pulling Kentucky Fried chicken legs out of their red-and-white box.

"We have to decide who goes with me and who goes with you."

I told Atta I could care less who was on my plane. They were all equally talented at throwing their weight around, and we were not talking long-lasting friendships, so what did it matter to me? "But I will not cut any throats," I said. "Sorry, I just can't. So give me men who are good with knives." Which was probably all of them.

Atta assigned me four men. I had no problem with them. But between us we only had seven men. We needed eight.

On that, Atta had news for me. "I am taking al-Omari. He is going to meet me down here a few days before we do it."

So Atta's "love affair" had become a plaited troth until death. "Okay." I couldn't help giggling. "That will work."


The chicken was gone. We washed our hands, performed the required salat and flopped on our beds to work out buying the one-way tickets.

I studied Atta's seating plan of the 767-200 as United Airlines had configured it. We had gotten it, and American's too, off the internet. There were ten seats in first class, in rows one and two. In each row there two on each side and one between the aisles. Behind first class was business class, rows five to ten; again, in each row there were two on each side, but here there were two center seats.

I did not want my men in first class to sit in the first row – the flight attendants could not help but be aware of them. The men who would sit in business class had to be located toward the back of the section for quick access to economy class, where their work would be.

I picked one man whom I knew could kill to sit in each of these sections, and paired each of them with another about whom I had some doubts. I assigned the two in first class to seats 2A and 2B, and the business class men to center seats, 9C and 9D. I would sit in 6C, between the two pairs of Saudis.

We would have to order the tickets soon to make sure that others did not steal the seats I planned to use. That work would begin tomorrow. It was almost midnight; I was through for the day.

Jarrah parked his flashy red Mitsubishi Eclipse and walked across A1A and up the Panther's outside stairs. He was still living in Lauderdale-By-The-Sea, but he would soon be going to Washington, where he and Hanjour would dole out their Saudis as Atta and I had done. Then Jarrah and the Saudis he chose would move up to New Jersey to get ready for their flight.

He was not smiling when he walked in – he was tense, concentrated, like a student stuffed with Dexedrine on the verge of a final exam. His face was drawn; he had lost some weight since I had seen him last. "Death to the Jews!" he grimaced. "Death to America!"

Atta, though, was more relaxed than I had ever known him to be. He was eating an Entenmann's donut, and he offered Jarrah one. Jarrah took it abstractedly and bit off tiny morsels.

"Have you flown lately, Jarrah?"

"I flew a check ride yesterday in Fort Lauderdale."

"You have to keep your skills up …"

"Don't worry about me, Atta. It comes naturally."

"Then let me tell you how to book the flights …"

"No." Jarrah waved Atta off. "I have been over to Germany, I went through it all with al-Shibh. I only came to say goodbye."

"It is not goodbye yet," Atta said. "I am going to come to Washington to make sure everything is all right."

Jarrah shrugged indifferently. "Is Marwan coming with you?"

"No."

"Well, I can say goodbye to Marwan, then." Jarrah reached out quickly and gripped my arm. "Walk with me to my car, okay? I have something for you."

Walking across A1A, neither of us spoke. But when he reached his car and pulled open the door, Jarrah cracked.

"I saw Aysel. My girlfriend. In Germany. I couldn't break it off. She knows me so well, she is so smart, she would have guessed I wouldn't do that unless something bad was coming."

"Maybe you just can't tell her …"

"No! I can't!" He leaned against a fender. He would have crumpled otherwise.

"You're going to let it be a surprise?"

"I told her I would be back soon … we would marry, start a family …"

"And have you been in touch with her …"

"I email or I call her almost every night."

I helped him to sit in the driver's seat. I leaned over him. "You are being very cruel," I said. "She'll be devastated …"

"Yes …"

I had a flash of insight I should have had much sooner. Or maybe I had had it earlier, but it hadn't registered. "Is it that you can't tell her ... or that there is nothing to tell?"

Jarrah knew what I meant. "Oh, shit, Marwan," he sobbed, "I don't want to end it with her."

There it was. The truth of it. "I asked you before, Ziad, if you were ready to do this. You're not. You have never been."

Jarrah looked up, sadly. "I wish I could be like you."

You are like me, I thought, in a way – and in another

way, you are not. It's love that is tearing you apart. I don't love anybody.

I leaned on my hands against the car and looked across the road at the Panther Motel. A skinny girl with brown hair was splashing in the pool. "You could make a run for it …"

"They will never leave me alone. Don't you have any doubts, Marwan? I mean, you're a happy guy …"

I watched the girl climb out of the Panther's pool. She peeled off her bikini top, threw on a Hard Rock T-shirt, sat down on a blue plastic chaise and stretched her long legs out.

I bowed my head for a moment. Then I said: "I'm going to do it, Ziad. It's what I'm supposed to do."


The next morning, two of my Saudis and two of Atta's, following my instructions, reserved seats over the internet in first class on each of the planes. Mine got the seats I had hoped for. Martyrdom was expensive: $4,500 a seat. One of them ordered a Muslim meal – no pork, sausage or animal fat, just lamb that had been slaughtered in Allah's name. He would never get to eat it, of course. Maybe he forgot.

The next day, Atta bought two seats, for himself and al-Omari, on a computer he rented time on at Kinko's Copy Shop. The day after that, my other Saudis bought business class seats in person at the airport in Fort Lauderdale. The day after that, I bought mine. It was August the 28th.

At nine o'clock Eastern time – three a.m. in Germany

– Atta called al-Shibh. It took a while for al-Shibh to answer. He would have been asleep.

"I have a question for you," Atta began. "A friend of mine gave me a puzzle, and I want you to help me out ... Yes, I know, it is very late, but only you could help me ... What is two sticks, a dash and a cake with a stick down?"

11-9.

In Europe, the day is written first, and after it, the month.

# 31

## Hollywood, Florida: September, 2001

The Newark and Washington crews were waiting for Atta at two motels a mile apart in Laurel, Maryland. Everything was according to plan. Jarrah was where he should be.

In a 7-Eleven parking lot in Falls Church, Virginia, Hanjour paid a hundred dollars to a man from El Salvador. The Latino took the Saudis who had been in Paterson to the nearby office of the Department of Motor Vehicles. He swore before a notary that his friends were Virginia residents. The DMV issued the Saudis identification cards. Those were the only documents the Saudis were going to need.

When Atta came back to Deerfield Beach, we left the Saudis at the Panther and moved to Hollywood once more, this time to a place called the Longwood Hotel. The Longwood must have been splendid in its day, but now, under its Spanish tile roof, it looked like a Mexican flophouse. On its ground floor there were two businesses: a downhearted consignment shop and a shabby "antique" store. The hotel's entranceway was narrow and dark. It looked threatening. Inside, it was not threatening, unless you are threatened by dirt.

Atta dispatched a FedEx package of items from his dufflebag that other men could use to an address in Dubai that al-Shibh had given him. I wired most of my money to a bank in the Emirates, keeping enough to pay the motels and to buy the Saudis' food. I wasn't hungry. I wasn't anything.

Those thoughts were getting at me again. I might wait at a "don't walk" sign, and forget what I was there for, until the people behind me pushed me into the street. I might be in the shower and not be aware of the water as it poured onto my head. I might be doing anything and just … for no reason … stop …

There was no language to the thoughts. They held no information. They did not suggest actions. They did not express regrets. I could not understand them. But I wasn't trying to; the good thing was, they kept me from comprehending things. They were a constant humming in the center of my skull, loosing waves of adrenalin to pour through my arteries.

But if these impulses were meaningless, the sensations were cataclysmic, a buzzing awfulness. I was leaning over a precipice; I was going to jump, I was going to feel the bones come apart and the muscles rip …

Atta saw what was happening. "You have to keep busy,

Marwan," he said. "Rent a video camera. Go up to Deerfield Beach. The Saudis may want to make statements – or something for their families."

"What?"

"Didn't you hear what I said?"

"No. Say it again."

Atta repeated himself. I started to laugh. "What are you going to do with the tapes? Take them on the planes?"

"I will mail them to someone. Do what I tell you, hah?"

I stopped at a store in Delray and rented a Panasonic. The Saudis were packing up their things when I arrived at the Panther.

I told them what I had come to do. The sight of the camera excited them – and that revolted me, as I am revolted by those women who shriek and scream and jump up and down when Al Roker comes out of the studio and leers at them. I would have shouted at the women: You *exist*, you fucking morons. You don't *have* to be on TV. It does not make you movie stars. You are still nobodies.

But the Saudis would not be nobodies after we did this thing. True, the Americans would not be able to pronounce their names and would not want to know who they were – they would not be individuals, just "Muslim fanatics;" not people, just "terrorists." But the Saudis did not care what the Americans knew. They would be heroes in the Islamic world, glorious martyrs – saints. And they wanted the rest of Islam, and their families, to realize why they had made the sacrifice, and to get the message that it was good and that more and more should follow them until the jihad was over and we had done away with the Jews.

I turned the camera on one of them. He grinned and waved sheepishly. He had seen Palestinian suicide tapes, but he could not duplicate those because he didn't have the toys – no vest packed with blocks of C-4, no Kalashnikov. He couldn't strike a martial pose with an X-acto knife. All he had was sincerity, and that does not work on video unless you have been trained to display it – you know, to put it across.

The others did no better, blah blah blah – except the last, who begged his mother to understand. I gave the tapes to Atta. I don't know what he did with them. I didn't make one, because there is no understanding this thing. There are only excuses that make it acceptable.

September 8, 2001. The Saudis were beginning to relocate to Boston. My crew were waiting for me at the Days Hotel in Brighton, on Soldiers Field Road along the Charles, just above Everett Square. Harvard was not far away, just across the river. The Saudis had heard of it. They walked across the Mass Ave bridge up to Harvard Square. Pretty girls, but too many Jews. They turned back.

Al-Omari had come to Hollywood the day before. There had been more of the mooning I had seen in Paterson. Al-

Omari seemed depressed; he was clinging onto Atta as if he would have to ride on Atta's back to get into Paradise – which, I suppose, was not far from the truth. His sweet face had lost its symmetry, as if some cerebral accident had relocated his eyes. He slept with Atta in Atta's bed and held him all night long.

Al-Omari and Atta were leaving the next day. They would be stopping first in New York; they would go down to the World Trade Center and, using Atta's GPS, check the towers' coordinates, which the man in Las Vegas had written out for Atta. Atta was going to call me and confirm the coordinates. He could not do that in person, because – if our plan went well – we were not going to see each other again.

From New York, they would fly to Boston and watch American 11's departure routine – how the flight was boarded, what sorts of people were on it, what the airline's ground personnel said to the passengers, what security measures seemed to be in effect. Then they would rent a car and drive to Portland, Maine. Atta had reserved a room at a Comfort Inn in South Portland. At six on the morning of the Day, they would ditch the car in the parking lot of the Portland International Jetport – it would not be due back in Boston until that night, so no one would be looking for it until it was too late – and catch a U.S. Airways commuter flight to Logan. The flight would take fifty minutes and arrive at Terminal B. The American flight to Los Angeles would be leaving from that terminal. They would have an hour and five minutes to find the American gate and get aboard the plane.

Atta had decided to do all this because he would be going through security at Portland, not at Logan. He knew Portland's security would be the less advanced – Portland had only one checkpoint, and it was a small regional airport, so its computer systems were less likely to be connected to any government watch lists. And he thought that if a flag went up when eight other Arabs tried to pass through Logan security, at least he would have a better chance of getting onto his flight. Whatever might happen to anyone else, he was not going to fail.

So he was abandoning me. He was very nervous about it, considering my state of mind, and the fact that it would be up to me to get myself and the rest of the Saudis to Boston and on the planes. He called Jarrah and al-Midhar. They were ready to go. So I was his final conundrum. I could ruin everything, and he thought I might.

At four o'clock, Atta was hungry. Al-Omari was, too. The last thing I wanted to do was eat, but Atta refused to leave me alone, he nagged at me until I agreed I would sit with them while they ate.

We walked only a short ways east into Young Circle, the hub of Hollywood nightlife, such as it was. Shuckums was a neighborhood seafood bar. There were sports pennants on one wall, on another a mural of the sea, and a huge stuffed shark. Four TVs hung behind the bar; the Marlins were losing to the

Mets on all four screens. You could sit in a polyurethaned pine booth or at the blue-trimmed bar, or at green plastic tables on the sidewalk under an awning. Later that night – it was Saturday – there would be a local band. But now it was just the beginning of Happy Hour. There were only three fishermen and three or four hard-faced blondes partying so far.

Atta took a barstool. Al-Omari and I followed him. Six elbows on the bar and three chins in three hands.

The bartender sauntered over. He was as bald as a cueball, and a half carat diamond stud glinted on each ear. "You eatin' or just drinkin'?"

Atta looked up at him. "I would like a menu, please."

The bartender whistled. A waitress in a short skirt brought three menus on a tray. I didn't look at the menu. Al-Omari couldn't read it. Atta scanned his quickly. "We'll have three orders of hot wings." The waitress gave him a big smile she surely did not mean. He didn't look at her. But I did.

There was no conversation. If there were anything we had to discuss, we could not discuss it there, and we had all moved beyond small talk for the rest of our lives.

I stared at the bottles behind the bar. I had never been a drinker. I barely knew what the labels meant, or what things tasted like. But this is a bad time, I thought: I am sitting here with nothing to do, and Allah would not begrudge me. I called the bartender over. "I would like something sweet, with liquor."

"We don't have a blender," the barman apologized. "I can mix ya a screwdriver."

"What is that?"

"Orange juice and vodka."

"That's okay."

And then al-Omari piped up. "I'll have a rum and coke."

The bartender studied Atta. "How about you?"

Atta looked at al-Omari and me, his eyebrows tied in knots. But he knew if he said a word to me he would have a fight on his hands. "Do you have any juice?"

"Just the mixin's – orange juice, pineapple, cranberry."

"Just .. I will take a cranberry juice."

The bartender grinned. "There's a good Moslem. These two boys are going to Hell!"

Atta's head snapped back and he braced himself. "What do you know about it?"

"Hey, this is Hollywood. I see Arabs smashed every night."

The food and the drinks came in one fell swoop. The chicken nauseated me; I pushed it away. But the orange drink in the tall glass glowed under the bar lights. I took a small sip. It tasted like morning in Ras al Khaimah – sweet, a little bitter. A large gulp went down effortlessly. I ordered another one. Al-Omari's rum and coke disappeared quickly, too.

Atta got up from the bar stool. He would not look at us. He walked to a pinball table not far away. He studied the instructions, then slipped a coin into a slot. Bells went off, lights flashed, numbers rolled over each other as Atta gripped a little knob and flipped a ball into play.

Four drinks and two hours later, Atta was still at the pinball machine. Al-Omari was giggling and swiping at his mouth. Two of the hard-faced blondes were across the bar from me. I leered at one of them – it didn't matter which: "Hey, sharmuta, how would you like to suck my zib?" I had never said anything like that before. I did not use that kind of language. But I liked using it.

"Suck your what?"

"Suck my dick! Katha ath nan!"

She got down off her barstool and walked towards me. "That depends on your dick," she said. "Let's have a look."

When she reached me, she unzipped my fly with a rope-veined hand. I glanced over at Atta. He would have liked to cut her throat. For the first time, I realized there was a murderer in him. I think he would have killed her if there were not bigger things to do.

The bartender leaned over and slapped her hand away. "Hey, not here!"

She curled a nostril at him. "Mon pére got a place on the beach," she said. "I don't have to hold back over there."

I was about to tell her that her Canuck shack sounded like just the environment I needed right now. But that I couldn't go there, because I had something to do … there was something that I had to do … But I didn't think I said any of that because the humming inside my head was forming syllables … I wasn't hearing them, I was seeing them. They were not red, they were blue … And the thing I have to do, honey, is DIE – I HAVE TO DIE!

The brows over the girl's blue eyes rolled up like window shades. Atta shoved her with the back of his arm, grabbed me by the front of my shirt and tore me away from her. Threw me into an empty booth, pinned me there, leaving al-Omari bleating at the end of the bar.

I couldn't breathe. I was not drunk anymore. The blood was blasting so hard through my veins it was going to breach their walls, and I was aware of the pressure on every inch of them. "Atta, I can't do it!"

"Marwan …" he sighed.

"*I cannot do this! I can't*!!"

But after a while I quieted down, and Atta let me loose. He reached into a pocket and brought a paper out. "Can you read?"

"What do you mean, can I read?"

"Can you read *now?*"

I was no longer quivering. "I don't want to read …"

"I wrote this for all of us. I have already given it to Jarrah and al-Midhar to give to their people on the night before. I was going to leave it for you. But I think it would be better if you read it now."

"What is it, a suicide note?"

"It is not for me. It's for you."

"I am not going to read it."

"Then I will read some of it to you. '*It is all right to be afraid. Everybody hates death, fears death, but only those, the believers who know the reward after death, would be the ones who will be seeking death.*'"

"Really." I shook my head. "Is that what you think?"

"'*Be calm and resolute*,'" Atta went on, "'*for soon you will be going to Paradise. You will be entering the happiest life, everlasting life. Know that the gardens have been decorated for you with the most beautiful ornaments, and that "the black-eyed" will call to you: "Come, faithful of Allah," after having donned their finest garments.*'"

"Seventy-two virgins," I said. "I can't wait."

He folded up the paper and slipped it into my pocket. "Have it your way, Marwan, then. Just remember what convinced you, and ask yourself what has changed."

The waitress clattered over with dirty dishes on a tray. "Hey, fellas, I'm goin' off shift – would ya mind payin' me now?"

"Kharra alaik," Atta snarled. Shit on you.

Her face turned mean and twisted. "All you Arabs are faggots. So take it up the ass!" She switched her behind all the way to the bar and whispered into the bartender's ear, pointing back at us.

223

"Atta," I asked, "when I was crazy, did I say anything to that blonde?"

"Yes, you said you had to die."

"Oh!" I marveled. "That's true."

The bartender came over with a heavy attitude. "Is there a money issue?"

Atta looked up, all innocence. "Kus umak." Your mother's cunt. "What is a money issue?"

"Do you have enough money to pay the tab?"

"I am a pilot for American Airlines. Of course I can pay the tab. How much is it?"

"Forty-eight bucks."

Atta pulled out a wad of currency, peeled off a hundred dollar bill. "Elhasi tizi." Lick my ass. He gave it to the man. When the waitress brought him back the change, he left a three dollar tip.

# 32

**Boston: September 9, 2001**

---

I had checked us out of the Panther, returned the rented car, sent the Saudis up to Boston and followed them myself. Some of them – they were Atta's – had a room outside the city at a motel in Chestnut Hill. I drove over to check on them as soon as I got in. The hotel was "budget level" – mold on the walls, water stains, cigarette holes in the sheets. There were wet washcloths left in the shower. But nobody cared.

The Saudis had pulled a bedspread down and laid it on the floor. They were in sujood – they were prostrate – chanting the subhanan laheh more than the three times prescribed, as if the phrase – "Glory to God!" – were the key to Paradise. Their eyes shone, and sweat dropped off their faces in rivulets. They were putting all they had into their entreaties to Allah, because at the last they had understood the dilemma they were in.

Unless it was Allah's will that they die on September 11th, they were doomed to failure, and worse, to Hell, because Allah had made it clear that no one dies except by His leave, at a time He predetermines. Martyrdom was glorious, but as the Prophet had said: *"If somebody kills himself with anything in this world, he will be tortured in Hell with that very thing on the Day of Resurrection."* If an infidel kills you in battle, you go to Paradise; but if you kill yourself to kill infidels, where do you go? Allah had not answered this question. The Saudis' chances at Paradise were at fifty-fifty odds.

Their voices were fervent – fervid. "Our Lord, do not condemn us if we make mistakes. Pardon us, forgive our transgressions, remit our sins, and let us be among the righteous when we die. Do not disgrace us on the Day of Resurrection. Admit us an honorable admittance and let us depart an honorable departure …"

I laid a copy of Atta's paper on a bed, and left them to finish their prayers.

The quandary had not occurred to the Saudis at the Days Hotel. They were quiet – it seemed they had concluded their emotional preparations. They had been driving to Logan daily to study the scene of the crime. I gave them Atta's paper. They did not look at it.

I wanted to walk the city that night, so I checked myself into the Milner Hotel on Charles Street, south of the Common. It was a down-at-the-heels brick building with dead window-box geraniums. The lobby and stairway were carpeted with a fire-engine red oriental. I could lay on the bed in the room I was given and touch two walls. But the tiny TV was functional, and I flipped on CNN. On the crawl at the bottom of the screen, I found interesting news.

Two men posing as journalists had killed Ahmad Shah Massoud, the chief of the so-called Northern Alliance in Afghanistan. There had been a bomb in their video camera. They had blown themselves up, too.

It was clear to me what had happened. Sheikh Usama had thought it was possible – even if Atta did not – that the Americans might go for him after we attacked. If they wanted to make a ground assault, they would need to use local fighters, the few men left of the many who had opposed the Taliban. The Sheikh had just killed the best of those men, the Lion of Panjshir. I wondered what else was going on that had to do with me.

I lay down on the coverlet and pulled out Atta's instructions. His handwriting was hard to read, but I made it out.

*For the last night:*

*Remind yourself that in this night you will face many challenges. But you have to face them and understand it one hundred percent. Completely forget something called "this life." The time of fun and waste has gone. The time of judgment has arrived. You should ask God for guidance, you should ask God for help. You should ask God for forgiveness. Continue to pray throughout this night. Continue to recite the Qur'an.*

I thought I would take that advice.

*And be optimistic. The Prophet was always optimistic.*

I thought I would try that, too.

*When you leave for the airport, make sure that you are clean, your clothes are clean, including your shoes. Tighten your shoes well, and wear socks that hold in the shoes and do not come out. Check around you before you leave. Make sure that no one is following you.*

That was Atta: attention to detail, to the point of absurdity.

*When you come aboard the airplane, don't show signs of tension; be joyful and happy, set your mind at ease, and be confident and rest assured that you are carrying out an action that Allah likes and that pleases Him.*

I did not think that I could manage that.

*When the airplane starts moving and heads toward takeoff, recite the supplication of travel, because you are traveling to God, may you be blessed in this travel. Say: "Oh God, open all doors for me. I am asking you to lighten my way. I am asking you to lift the burden I feel."* I know what that burden will be – the burden of fear.

How perceptive, cousin. But *you* won't be afraid. "The pain lasts only a second," you said. "After that, it is bliss."

*Fear God, if you are believers. For fear is a great act of worship that can be offered only to God, and He is most worthy of it.*

*Remember to make your knife sharp, and not to discomfort*

*the animal when you slaughter it.*

*Obey God and his Messenger, and stand fast. Praise Allah and hold out your chest as the plane goes into the building. We are of God, and to God we return.*

# 33

**Boston: September 9, 2001**

---

But an hour of asking God for help was as much as I could manage. The room was closing in on me. It felt like a sarcophagus. So I left the hotel and walked up Charles Street toward Beacon Hill, turned onto Boylston Street, then onto Arlington. It was a glorious late summer night. An easy breeze was blowing in off Massachusetts Bay.

I strolled past the shops on Newbury Street through hordes of college students on the hunt for mates to keep them warm when the city grew cold and gray. Every yuppie American must-have was for sale in the elegant rows of townhouses with high front stoops: art, antiques, high-end clothes, hair salons and day spas, plastic surgeons and in the restaurant windows plates of food juxtaposing bright colors like sculptural Mirós. I heard snatches of conversation that betrayed intellect in the midst of all the "Omigod"s and "duh!"s and "like"s and "awesome!"s.

Passing by a bookstore, I turned in. I needed to find something to keep me occupied. If that were possible.

The books – new and used – on the wooden shelves were an eclectic collection, but if I had a fancy left, there was nothing there to strike it. There were magazines, too, and I thumbed through those. Tables full of bonsai trees, tarot cards and incense. And then I noticed a small shelf of imported CDs. I was curious what I might find there. I could buy a Walkman. I missed my rock and roll.

A girl in a white tank top and hip-hugging jeans was standing in front of the shelf. I stood on my tiptoes behind her – she was tall – and looked over her shoulder past her lush black hair. Her fingers were deliciously long, and she was balancing on the tips of them a Rachid Taha CD.

"Do you like him?" I asked.

"Yeah. He turns me on. He's so intense and guttural."

"Do you understand what he is singing about?"

"No – but I think it's about anger … and respect."

She turned and let me look at her. Her face was full, but the bones were well-placed; her lips were like Angelina Jolie's, and she had Sandra Bullock eyes that shone with intelligence.

"You're beautiful," she said.

I turned red. "You're so dark," I said. "Do you have Arab blood?"

"Summer in Nantucket," she laughed. "You're Arab? Where are you from?"

"Ras al Khaimah. It is one of the Emirates."

"Buy me a cappuccino and describe it for me."

I ordered two of the coffees at the bookstore's long beverage bar. She stood next to me, the flesh of her arm brushing mine lightly once in a while.

"Do you know where the Emirates are?"

"Yes, I do." We carried our tiny cups to a table by the windows that looked out on Newbury Street.

"Ras al Khaimah is on the Persian Gulf. On the Ru'us al-Jibal peninsula. It is very small. It's desert. The khamsin – the hot wind – blows over it. My father's people are Shohor – Bedu, you know Bedu?"

"Yes."

"From the mountains outside the city. They don't leave the mountains much. They don't talk to strangers."

"But you do."

"My family was different. We lived in town. And my mother is Egyptian. They will talk to anybody."

She laughed – it was magical, with the milk froth on her lips. "Oh, God! What school are you at?"

"Harvard," I said, thinking quickly. "The … uh … Urban Planning School." Did Harvard even have one? "How about you?"

"Emerson."

"I don't know Emerson."

"Oh, who does? It's a communications program. I major in journalism."

"You want to be a reporter?"

"I want to do TV."

"I think you would be very good at it."

"Yes, I think I would." Until then, she had not taken her eyes off mine. Now they dipped for a morsel of modesty, and then flipped up and locked me again. I had never known anyone like her.

"Do they let women do TV in Ras al Khaimah?" she asked.

"Yes. Now they do. We are very sophisticated."

She was silent for a second. Then she made up her mind. "I'm cooking dinner tonight. Want to come?"

I didn't answer. I knew I should not have been doing this.

"You won't have to talk to strangers, it will be just you and me."

"What time is dinner?"

"As soon as I get it made."

She grabbed my hand and tugged me out into the street. "Gotta pick up a few things. What can't you eat?"

"In America I eat everything."

"That's nice of you."

She skittered the length of Newbury Street. She bought tenderloins and vegetables at DeLuca's Back Bay Market; aromatherapy candle columns at Diptyque. Next door to the bookshop was Condom World. "Just in case," she grinned. She picked out what they call "teasers." "I love these."

"When will you tell me your name?" I asked.

"It's Tallulah. Can you believe it?"

"It's what?"

"It's Carol, okay?"

"Don't you want to know my name?"

"I will, I think," she murmured. "But not yet."

She had a first floor apartment in a brownstone on Beacon Street. The geraniums in her window boxes were well cared for. From the high ceilings and windows it looked like someone rich had put up the building, and from the furnishings I concluded that someone rich lived in it now. "Like all the doodads?" she said. "That's mom and dad. All *I* need are a pillow and an ice cream scoop."

She was from Minnesota, she said, as she chopped her scallions. The candles sent up tranquil curls of scent. Her father was a surgeon, did heart transplants. Her brother Jack was an itinerant surfer bum. She had been valedictorian of her high school class. "And then you get to Boston, and everybody's smart."

"But not everybody is beautiful … "

"Shhh! We are not supposed to mention that!" She tossed her choppings into a large cast-iron skillet. "Boston women want men to want them for their minds. But there isn't a man in this world who wants a woman for her mind. Do men want women for their minds in Ras al Khaimah?"

"Actually, they do – but not in the way you mean it."

"Men might want to *use* your mind – to their own advantage, of course – but that isn't why they keep you around. And they only want to use your mind if it works like a man's. I don't see anything wrong with that. That's just how it is. Like, business is a male thing. You have to think like them. If your brain works like a woman's, you better look pretty damn good, or you better be doing research in some little lab in the basement of Harvard or MIT. Or writing ditzy literature. Otherwise you're hopeless. You're just fucked."

"But I like the way women think …"

She scoffed. "They don't think. They emote."

"You think. I can see it."

"Don't tell anyone, okay? But you know," she sighed, "I can go all to pieces for the most godawful reasons." She looked up from the meat she was seasoning. "You could make me do that. Couldn't you."

"You know," I said, "I think that is what you are doing to me." It was true. She was unsettling me. I should not let this go on.

She dropped her fork and snaked her arms around my neck. "Don't get squirrelly, what's-your-name. I am not one of those women who needs to be on top." The kiss she gave me then was as soft as a goosedown pillow, except for the little nip on the lip that signaled the end of it.

She popped the steaks into the skillet. I studied each of the little hairs that straggled down her nape. "I am good at this, you know?" she said. She was very good at this.

She was delicate the first time. She kept stopping me and holding me back until we had completely understood each sensation we brought each other to. The next time she wanted ferocity – and I had that in me. The third time she wanted tenderness. Then she drew her counterpane over me and let me sleep.

# 34

**Boston: September 10, 2001**

---

When the sun slashed through her windows, showing us another beautiful day, she slipped out of bed in nothing. Her body, backlit through her sheers, was as breathtaking as her face. She was in her kitchen a moment. She returned with a bowl of cubed green melons and pineapple chunks. "I was thinking of an oasis," she grinned. "But I don't have any dates."

We fed the fruit to each other a while, then rubbed it on each other, licking off the juice, until other juices were flowing again and she giggled: "I didn't say never on top," as she threw herself over me.

She had just stepped out of the shower. She was wrapping her hair in a terrycloth towel as she sashayed over to me. She had pretty nearly crippled me. I could not get out of bed. "Poor

239

baby," she said. "But hey, I blew off two classes this morning for you. What about you?" I told her I had none scheduled. "I'm open this afternoon," she said. "Got anywhere to go?"

I thought: I had better get out of there. But I said "No."

"What do you want to do?" she asked. "Besides more of the same. Which is not what I meant when I said I would be open this afternoon."

"You can show me Boston."

"You haven't seen it yet?"

"I've only been here two days."

"Okay. I'll run you a shower."

"No. I do not want to wash you off me. Ever."

She stopped moving and stared at me. Her face was suddenly soft. "That is the sweetest thing anyone has ever said to me."

I said: "I can think of nicer things to say …"

She put a finger across her lips. "Hold those off a while."


We wandered across the Common, holding hands. The light was sharp, like early fall; the air was startlingly clear. Fast-moving men in business suits and ambling women with babies clogged the paths that ran through the park. We kissed every ten seconds as we walked across the grass.

When the grass ran out at the park's eastern edge, we headed up Tremont Street past the Emerson campus, which she proudly pointed out; then turned right on State Street, by new and stolid old banks. When we veered into Merchants' Row, there was a long low building ahead with a glassed-in arcade.

"What is this place?" I asked her.

"Quincy Market. I thought you would like to see it. It's sort of a shopping mall."

We turned to the left and walked between two of these long low buildings on a promenade paved with red brick and cobblestones. There seemed to be dozens of pushcarts and shops filled with junk, and thousands of tourists with cameras, in Mickey Mouse T's or Birkenstocks or L.L. Bean's.

America, I said to myself. Full of crap.

At the end of the promenade was a three-story brick building topped with a square wooden steeple with a four-sided clock. "Do you know American history?" she asked.

"A little bit."

"This was a produce market, going all the way back. Sam Adams used to speak here. He used to stir up the crowd."

"For your American revolution? Yes, I know about that."

On the other side of the building, in an open square, Samuel Adams stood in brass on a concrete pedestal, dressed in eighteenth-century style with his arms folded over his chest. I went around to the front of him and read the words carved under his feet:

> HE ORGANIZED THE REVOLUTION
> AND SIGNED THE
> DECLARATION OF INDEPENDENCE

Was it just accident that I happened, right at that moment, to see those words – or did Allah move Carol to put me there? It did not matter which was true – the result, in either case, would have been the same. I put an end to the tenderness. As I had known I would have to do.

"Do you know the words of your Declaration of Independence?" There was a slicing edge to my voice. She looked at me quizzically.

"I think I do," she answered. "Some of them, anyway."

"So maybe you can explain something to me." She stopped and turned to look at me. She knew there was trouble coming.

"The words say that all men are created equal by God, and God gives all men the right to live, the right to be free and to try to find happiness. This language is simple – and who would disagree? But do these words mean to Americans what the dictionary says they mean? For example: Does it mean men only? Because you women could not vote until the twentieth century."

"What are you doing?" she asked me, her eyes growing sad.

"Does it mean all American white men? Because the niggers do not have these rights …"

She bristled. "Don't call them that!"

"Why not? That is what they call themselves. And us they call "sand niggers," so I can call them what I want. Or does it mean what it says – *all* men – everyone in the world? Because

242

that is not the way you behave. You don't care about anyone's happiness except your own.

"You support dictators. You support corrupt regimes. You support apostate kings and sultans in Muslim lands. You support rulers the people do not want, who crush the poor. Any people who go for freedom, you smash them down – if you can. You support bloodsucking oppressors. Look at Palestine! My people suffer! And all of it is to make yourselves rich at everyone else's expense!"

"Look, some of that is true …"

"You are studying journalism. You know all of it is true! And then this declaration says that when a government proves by what it does that it is a despotism, it is the people's duty to get rid of that government."

She was afraid of me. She was backing away.

"Why should only Americans have that right? If your government is despotic, shouldn't *all men*, anyone in the world, have the right to bring it down? Is that not what you claimed to do – in Bosnia, in Somalia? And those governments had no effect on you – but you, you affect everybody!"

"Oh, God," she sighed. "What a fucked-up world."

And then my cell phone rang.

"Where are you?" It was Bulbul, the nightingale.

"In Boston. Walking around."

"I just got to where I was going. Is everything all right?"

"It is as far as I know."

"You had better know better than that!"

"Okay, okay, I'll check on them."

"Jarrah almost ruined it. They sent his airline ticket to Florida. He gave them that address. He had to drive down and get it."

"Why didn't he fly?"

"I don't know," Atta said. But I think *I* did.

"He got pulled over in Maryland. He was going ninety miles an hour on I-95. Thank God he had a license, or who knows where he would be? Anyway, he is in Newark. Just breathing a little hard."

"I am very glad to hear it," I said.

"Are you going crazy again?"

I was, I thought – but that's over now. "No. Are you?"

"Are you afraid Marwan?"

"*What do you think?*"

Atta's voice was suddenly soothing. Comfortable. "Death is like sleeping. I promise you. You will have good dreams. And the time between death and resurrection passes like one night."

"*Bullshit! Bullshit! Bullshit!*"

"Get hold of yourself, Marwan!"

"*Kharra alaik!*"

The girl is watching me, and I am berserk.

"Marwan, Marwan," Atta cooed. "I tell you the truth. I know what I am talking about. I don't say what I don't know."

I panted into the mouthpiece, like a stupid dog choked from straining against his chain. "I will never forgive you …"

"Be quiet, Marwan. Say Allah's ninety-nine names. And do not forget to get New York weather before you go. There is a number for pilots that you can call. An automatic service. I will call you tomorrow. One more time."

I punched the button, put away the phone. Carol was crying. "It isn't my fault," she said.

But it *was* her fault. No one is innocent. Do something or do nothing – the guilt is the same.

"Carol, I have things to do. I have to go."

"What happened?" she whimpered. "I don't understand."

I touched her chin, lifted it. "Look ….. Never mind."

"What … why …what?" she said. But I was walking away.

"Hey!" she yelled after me. "What the fuck is your name?"

# 35

**Boston: September 10, 2001**

---

Two hookers were walking out of the Saudis' room in the Days Hotel, wiping their lips with tissues and spitting on the floor.

"He wanted to fuck me up the ass!" one complained to the other. "Jesus Christ! Did you see the size of his dick?"

"Uh uh, I couldn't," the other said. "You were swallowing it."

"Knocked my fucking bridgework loose. He woulda split me in half!"

"Hello, ladies!" I said.

"Shit! Another one!" They hurtled down the hallway, their arms and legs pumping like speed-walkers as they sped toward the lobby, away from me.

The Saudis were sitting like yogis on the beds. I sat down beside one of them. "Is there anything you need?"

"Maaleesh," he smiled. Never mind. "Now we are

prepared. Kul shay fi yad Allah. What will happen is qadar. It is preordained."

"Ana mabsut beshughlak," I said. I am happy with your work.

I told them I would pick them up in the morning at six. The Saudi reached out and gripped my hand. "Shukhran, saddiq. We are going to pray now. Will you pray with us?"

"No," I said. "I have to check on Atta's crew."

"Entabeh." Be careful, the Saudi said. "Maasalaama." Goodbye.

The men at the Chestnut Hill hotel were on their knees again. Or maybe they had never been off them since I had seen them the night before. "Kefayeh!" I said. "That's enough!" But they did not agree.

"Tomorrow, leave here for the airport at six o'clock," I said. "It may take an hour to get there, or maybe less. Park in short term parking in the central parking lot. Go to Terminal B. Check in curbside. Get your boarding passes there. Go through security. Remember what Atta wrote you: be relaxed.

"When you have cleared security, scatter into the shops. Stand by the doorways. Do not be obvious about it. And keep a watch for Atta walking by. When he sees you, he will signal you what to do.

"If they call your flight and you have not seen Atta yet, go to the gate one at a time and get on board. If he misses the flight, mush kuwayis! Do nothing! Inta fahamt? None of you can fly the plane. There is nothing you can do."

I stood. "That is all I can tell you. The rest is in Allah's hands."

One of the Saudis nodded. I assumed he understood.

The New York METAR weather report at John F. Kennedy Airport, early morning, 11 September, 2001: It was going to be a perfect day.

I did not try to sleep that night. Did not want to sleep. But what could you think of on your last night that did not make it worse? Carol's smell was still on me. I scrubbed it off in the shower, scrubbed the whole world off. Then I put on tomorrow's clothes, and began with the Bismillah ….

# 36

## Boston: September 11, 2001

We could not find a parking space when the Days Inn Saudis and I pulled in to Logan's short term lot. We had hit heavy traffic coming in from Brookline along Boylston Street. It was already seven o'clock. The Saudis were building up steam.

Along the row ahead of us, I saw a Ford Explorer beginning to back out of a space. There was a little white Toyota standing by to pull into it. On its back bumper was a sticker: "LIFE IS SHORT. PRAY HARD." I whipped my car past both of them, then threw it into reverse. I cut off the Toyota and backed into the space.

The Toyota driver jumped out, ready to pound on me. The Saudis got out of the car and surrounded him. One of the Saudis grabbed him by the throat. "You know what it says on your bumper?" I growled. "Better start now." The Toyota man swallowed hard, then submissively turned around and slumped back to his car. I told the Saudis, as Toyota man drove off: "After the plane gets in the air, when I stand up, it begins."

We ran through the parking lot, dragging our bags, rode up the elevator from Departures to Arrivals and walked unhurriedly outside to the curbside check-in stand. We were asked the stupid questions. It was easy. So was security.

It was almost 7:30. We would board at 7:45. The sky was bright blue, like yesterday. I sat in a row of leather chairs and watched CNN. Out in the rest of the world, nothing important was going on.

People used to dress to fly. It was a special occasion. They used to sit in comfortable seats, attended by beautiful women in uniforms by Dior, spread linen napkins on their laps and eat chateaubriand. Now they are all in sneakers and jeans, muscle shirts, halter tops with their tits hanging out, the droopy drawers the schvartzen thought up that all the white kids wear, fat old women in jump suits with their hair dyed a brassy blonde and cut like a football helmet, and these guys in shorts and T-shirts with their bellies full of beer. The flight attendants are grandmothers, or they're gay. Flying isn't special now. It's like riding a bus.

"We'll begin by boarding our first class passengers." Two of the Saudis slowly stood, hoisted up their carry-ons and walked casually to the gate, taking places in the line several passengers back. When they started boarding business class, I did the same. I handed my boarding pass to a slightly disheveled girl. She tore off the end of it. "Have a nice flight!" she said.

The Saudis had already buckled in when I went past them down the aisle. Their eyes were downcast, and I could see their lips moving rhythmically. I could not hear the words, but I knew what they were saying, because I had spoken the same words at four o'clock in the morning: faraj, and the declaration of faith, the prayers before death.

I took my seat, 6C, behind them in business class. The man in the seat beside me looked to be in his thirties. He seemed like a laptop guy. He would not be a talker. We did not acknowledge each other as I sat down.

I pushed my carry-on under the seat and fastened my belt. The other two Saudis passed me. We avoided each others' eyes. A man with a beach ball belly leaned into me, trying to stuff a shopping bag into the compartment above my head. It wouldn't fit, and he wouldn't quit; his penis was nudging my shoulder, and he didn't apologize. A fury built up inside me; I could have ripped his heart out, if I had had a knife.

My cell phone rang. "Where are you?"

"I'm on the plane."

"We are on the taxiway. The plane from Portland came in late. We almost missed the flight. We were running through the terminal, I don't know what we looked like. I was sure they were going to stop us. I have to calm myself."

Atta paused. I didn't say anything. "Hello? Marwan? Are you there?"

"I don't have anything to say."

"Say your prayers."

"Atta – tell me about your girlfriend. You said you had a girlfriend once. Tell me about her."

"Not now, Marwan!"

"No? Then when?"

"…. She … she was a Palestinian girl. I met her in Aleppo. She worked in the Planning Bureau, that's how we met. She was very beautiful, and very bright. She was a good Muslim – you know, took taxis instead of buses, to stay away from men. Really she could not afford it, but she did. We saw each other very much, almost every day, while I was in Aleppo. She could talk about things I cared about. She liked to kiss me. She called me a Pharoah once; I think that was good."

"Did you love her?"

"Oh – who can say? She wanted too much freedom. I could not … you know … so … and then my father said: 'A Palestinian? A refugee? This is very bad, Mohammad!'"

A stewardess bent over me and smiled. "You'll have to shut that phone off now."

"Okay," I said, as politely as I could.

# About the Author

Aram Schefrin is the author of four novels. He is a pioneer in the new art of podcasting fiction, and this novel can be downloaded from iTunes and heard in its entirety. Mr. Schefrin practices law in Rhode Island and Florida. He was a founding member and the lyricist of the rock group Ten Wheel Drive, which had its moment of fame in the early 1970's. He lives in Wellington, Florida with his wife, two dogs, four cats and three polo ponies.

59102843R00161